Welcome to the November 2008 collection of
Harlequin Presents! What better way to warm up
in the coming winter months than with a hot novel
from your favorite Presents author—and this month
we have plenty in-store to keep you cozy! Don't miss
Ruthlessly Bedded by the Italian Billionaire
by Emma Darcy, in which a case of mistaken identity
leads Jenny Kent to a billionaire's bed. Plus, be sure
to look out for *The Sheikh's Wayward Wife,*
the second installment of Sandra Marton's fantastic
trilogy THE SHEIKH TYCOONS, and Robyn Donald's
final story in her brilliant MEDITERRANEAN PRINCES
duet, *The Mediterranean Prince's Captive Virgin.*

Also this month, read the story of sexy Italian
Joe Mendez and single mom Rachel in *Mendez's
Mistress* by favorite author Anne Mather. And in
Kate Walker's *Bedded by the Greek Billionaire,*
a gorgeous Greek seeks revenge on an English rose—
by making her his mistress! Vincenzo is intent
on claiming his son from estranged wife Emma
in *Sicilian Husband, Unexpected Baby* by
Sharon Kendrick, while Susan Napier brings you
Public Scandal, Private Mistress, in which
unsuspecting Veronica becomes involved with
billionaire Luc. Finally, in Ally Blake's *A Night with the
Society Playboy,* Caleb wants just one more night with
the woman who walked out on him ten years ago....

We'd love to hear what you think about Presents.
E-mail us at Presents@hmb.co.uk or join in the
discussions at www.iheartpresents.com and
www.sensationalromance.blogspot.com, where you'll
also find more information about books and authors!

VIVA LA VIDA DE AMOR!

They speak the language of passion.

In Harlequin Presents, we bring you a special kind of lover, oozing Latin charm and sexiness! He *knows* how to treat his woman, and he'll sweep you off your feet. He's got spirit, style and sex appeal!

Latin Lovers from Harlequin Presents is the miniseries for anyone who enjoys hot romance!

Anne Mather

MENDEZ'S MISTRESS

TORONTO • NEW YORK • LONDON
AMSTERDAM • PARIS • SYDNEY • HAMBURG
STOCKHOLM • ATHENS • TOKYO • MILAN • MADRID
PRAGUE • WARSAW • BUDAPEST • AUCKLAND

ISBN-13: 978-0-373-12773-3
ISBN-10:   0-373-12773-1

MENDEZ'S MISTRESS

First North American Publication 2008.

All about the author...
Anne Mather

I've always wanted to write—which is not to say I've always wanted to be a professional writer. On the contrary, for years I wrote only for my own pleasure, and it wasn't until my husband suggested that I send one of my stories to a publisher that we put several publishers' names into a hat and pulled one out. The rest, as they say, is history. And now, more than 150 books later, I'm literally staggered by what happened.

I had written all through my childhood and on into my teens, the stories changing from children's adventures to torrid gypsy passions. My mother used to gather these up from time to time, when my bedroom became too untidy, and dispose of them! The trouble was, I never used to finish any of the stories, and *Caroline,* my first published book, was the first book actually completed. I was newly married then, and my daughter was just a baby, and it was quite a job juggling my household chores and scribbling away in exercise books every chance I got. Not very professional, as you can imagine, but that's the way it was.

I now have two grown-up children—a son and daughter—and two adorable grandchildren, Abigail and Ben. My e-mail address is mystic-am@msn.com, and I'd be happy to hear from any of my readers.

CHAPTER ONE

'HE WAS everything a woman might ever want in a man: tall, dark, ruthless good looks masking a dangerous will that had made him a millionaire before his twenty-fifth birthday. He sat beside her on the sofa, too close for comfort, and oozing the kind of blatant sexuality that weakened her defences. Power and determination had made him successful in business, but Lavender had no intention...'

'I don't have to go if you don't want me to, Mum.'

Rachel had been lost in the intriguing love life of her latest heroine when Daisy appeared in her office doorway, but her daughter's words brought a crushing end to that imaginary world.

'Oh, Daisy!' Rachel exclaimed, getting up from her desk to give the girl a swift hug. 'When did I say I didn't want you to go?'

'You didn't,' said Daisy, recoiling from her mother's embrace with all the youthful independence of a thirteen-year-old. 'But I know what you think of Lauren. I don't like her much either. And the last time I visited them they were still living in England.'

Rachel sighed. She was always amazed at Daisy's capacity to understand her feelings. She wasn't always amenable. Like any teenager her age, she and her mother didn't always see eye to eye. But where her father was concerned, there was no contest.

Daisy had known that his invitation to spend at least two weeks of her summer holidays with him and his second wife at their home in Florida could prove controversial. For the first three years of his marriage to Lauren, Steve had only seen his daughter a handful of times, even though Rachel had agreed to share custody. But suddenly, since Steve's move to the company's headquarters in Miami last year, he'd been eager to have her spend every holiday with him.

Rachel hadn't voiced any objections. She wanted Daisy to know her father. But there was still a twinge of apprehension at the thought that Daisy might find life in the United States far more exciting than living here in Westlea, a quiet English country town.

'Look, I don't mind,' she assured Daisy now, refusing to consider how she would feel if Daisy did decide to live with her father. Rachel's unexpected success in recent years as a romantic novelist had proved satisfying, but it certainly wouldn't compensate for the loss of her daughter as well as her husband.

'Well…' Daisy still looked doubtful, and Rachel wanted to hug her again. 'If you're sure?'

'You'll have a lovely time,' said Rachel, unable to resist tucking a strand of dark hair behind her daughter's ear. She paused. 'I just wish your father hadn't arranged for you to travel across the Atlantic with some strange man.'

Daisy laughed then. 'He's not a strange man, Mum,' she protested. 'I have met him before. When Daddy lived in London. He's his boss, actually. His family owns Mendez Macrosystems. Lauren really likes him. I know she thinks he's hot.'

Rachel's jaw dropped. 'Hot?'

'Yeah.' Daisy stared at her. 'Duh. As opposed to boring? Honestly, Mum,' she grimaced, 'if you're writing for a modern audience you ought to know these things.'

'I know.' Rachel was defensive. 'But what makes you think Lauren regards this man as *hot*?' She pulled a face. 'For heaven's sake, she and your father have only been married for four years.'

'And your point is?' Daisy was sardonic. 'Oh, Mum, get real, will you? Women like Lauren are always on the lookout for the next good thing.'

Rachel shook her head. 'I don't think we should be having this conversation, Daisy.'

'Why not?'

'Well…because Lauren is your father's wife.'

'You were Daddy's wife when she decided she wanted him,' pointed out Daisy shrewdly. 'Honestly, Mum, I don't know what you're worried about. If she and Dad get a divorce, you and he could get back together.'

Could they?

Rachel didn't answer her, aware that that option was no longer as attractive as it might once have been. Experience had taught her that Steve Carlyle was not and had never been the man she thought she'd married. Lauren Johansen hadn't been the first female to attract Steve's attention during the nine years of their relationship. She'd just been the richest, and the most determined.

'Anyway, you'll get to meet him yourself before we go,' Daisy went on, reverting back to their earlier discussion. 'Mr Mendez, I mean. When he picks me up to take me to the airport.' She dimpled. 'Wait until I get back and tell Joanne. She'll be so hacked off. I can't wait.'

Rachel groaned. '"Hacked off"? Daisy, what kind of language is that?'

'Okay, green with envy, then, is that better?' Daisy pulled a face. 'Like I say, Mum, you really need to update your vocabulary.'

'Not with words like that,' said Rachel a little prudishly,

and then, realising she wasn't going to get any more work done that morning, she switched off her computer and followed her daughter out the door. 'Anyway, it's lunchtime. Do you want an omelette or a salad?'

'Couldn't I have a ham-and-cheese toastie?' asked Daisy wheedlingly. Lately, since she'd got her period, she was inclined to put on weight rather too easily, and Rachel was trying to wean her onto a healthier diet.

'I suppose so.'

Rachel was pragmatic. Daisy was unlikely to stick to eggs and salads while she was on holiday, so what was one sandwich more or less? Which reminded her, they only had five days before Daisy left for Florida. A depressing thought.

Daisy was due to spend the following day with her grand-parents. Steve's mother and father had never approved of their son's behaviour, and as Rachel's parents had died in a car accident when she'd only been a teenager herself, she and the elder Carlyles had always been very close. It meant Rachel would have a whole day to try and catch up with her deadline, which had definitely floundered since Daisy had accepted her father's invitation.

Consequently, she was irritated when the doorbell rang just after eleven o'clock that morning. She wasn't expecting any visitors. There were no edited manuscripts on their way back to her for approval, so it was unlikely to be the postman. And her neighbours knew better than to interrupt her before twelve o'clock.

Getting up, she went across to her office window and looked out. She was seriously considering not answering the door, but the sight of a powerful black SUV standing at her gate caused her to revise her opinion. Who on earth did she know who owned a vehicle like that?

No one.

And then a man stepped back from the shadow of the

overhang and looked up directly at her window. A dark man, she saw, with hair cut so short it was barely more than stubble over his scalp. It was difficult to judge how tall he was from this angle, but Rachel got the impression of height and power, broad shoulders encased in an age-scuffed leather jacket.

She stepped behind the curtain automatically, not wanting him to think she was spying on him, but it was too late. He'd seen her. The second peal of the bell proved it, and with a rapidly beating heart she left her office and hurried downstairs.

As she unlocked the door, she wondered if she was being entirely wise. After all, she was alone here. She didn't know this man, and he certainly looked as if he was no stranger to trouble.

But that was her novelist's imagination taking over, she thought impatiently. He was stranger, yes, but he'd probably picked the wrong address. He might be looking for someone. Julie Corbett, for example. Her flirtatious neighbour two doors down definitely attracted a lot of male attention. The kind of male attention this man had in spades.

She opened the door a few inches, making sure to keep most of her body hidden. Her strappy vest and shorts were not for public consumption, not when she was sure her hips spread every time she sat down at her desk. 'Can I help you?'

The man—she'd been right, he was tall: easily six feet, with a lean, muscled build—grinned at her. His face was darkly tanned, almost swarthy, with well-defined cheekbones, dark, hooded eyes, and a nose that looked as if it might have been broken at some time. He wasn't handsome, as the men she wrote about were handsome, but she had to admit that tough, masculine features and a hard thin-lipped mouth were infinitely more sexy. He was also younger than she was, she decided. But that didn't prevent him from embodying the kind of power and authority that made her catch her breath.

God!

'Rachel,' he said, shocking her still further by his casual use of her name. 'It is Rachel, isn't it?'

Rachel swallowed. 'Should I know you?' she asked faintly, sure that they'd never met before, and he pulled a wry face.

'No,' he said, his accent definitely not English. 'But I know your daughter. Daisy?' And when that aroused no immediate recognition, 'I'm Joe Mendez.'

Rachel felt weak. This surely couldn't be the man who owned Mendez Macrosystems—Steve's boss! It didn't seem possible. Weren't company executives supposed to wear three-piece suits, and ties and lace-up Oxfords? Not black leather jackets over tee shirts and jeans, and sockless loafers that had seen better days.

'I—Daisy's not here,' she said lamely, and Joe Mendez propped a hand against the wall beside the door and regarded her with the same look of tolerance her daughter sometimes employed.

'I didn't come to see Daisy,' he said, glancing behind him at the SUV. 'Is it okay leaving the car there?'

Which seemed to denote an expectation of being invited in. Rachel hesitated. 'It's a quiet road,' she said. Indeed, few unfamiliar vehicles entered the cul-de-sac. 'Um—what can I do for you, Mr Mendez?'

'Joe,' he corrected her evenly. He glanced pointedly over her shoulder. 'May I come in?'

'Oh…' Well, why not? she argued frustratedly. It wasn't as if he was a complete stranger, and she owed it to Daisy to be polite. She stepped back, remembering, as her bare feet protested the chill of the hall tiles, that she was hardly dressed for visitors, but it was too late to think of that now. 'Of course.'

'Thanks.'

Joe stepped into the hall, immediately filling it with his presence, and, leaving him to close the door, Rachel led the way into a rather formal sitting room. It was rarely used, and in spite of the mildness of the day it had a cool, impersonal feel. But she could hardly take him into the kitchen-cum-breakfast room where she and Daisy spent most of their time, could she?

He stood in the doorway, surveying the room, and Rachel gestured rather offhandedly towards the sofa. 'Please, sit down.'

He smiled, slightly uneven white teeth adding to his sensual appeal. Rachel knew she'd never encountered a man like him before and, remembering what Daisy had said, she could quite see why Lauren might think he was 'hot'.

She was relieved when he moved into the room and took a seat on the sofa, although he didn't appear to relax. He sat on the edge of the cushions, legs spread, hands hanging loosely between. And, when he looked up at her with a slightly whimsical expression, Rachel knew he was perfectly aware of the effect he was having on her.

Which made it easier, somehow. If she could just convince herself that she wasn't like all those other women who lusted after him—Lauren, for example—she could handle this.

'Coffee?' she asked brightly, overwhelmingly conscious of her exposed midriff and bare legs. 'I usually make myself a cup at this time of the morning.'

'Sounds good.'

He was easy, and Rachel offered him a smile before quickly exiting the room. Had she time to dash upstairs and put on trousers and a shirt? she wondered as she hurried into the kitchen. But no. That would just be pandering to his conceit, and if you turned up unexpectedly you should be prepared to take people as you found them.

She'd filled the container before going up to work, so all she had to do was turn on the coffee maker. Within seconds the comforting suck and slurp of the filter filled the air and, with a careless shrug, she turned to take two mugs from the wall cupboard above the counter.

'Daisy told me you're a writer,' said Joe Mendez from

behind her, and Rachel almost dropped the cups. Without any apparent sound, he'd left the sitting room and was now standing at the bar where she and Daisy usually ate their breakfast. He'd shed his leather jacket to reveal a tight-fitting body shirt and jeans that rode low on his lean hips, and Rachel couldn't help a certain twinge of resentment that he'd felt relaxed enough to make himself at home.

'Oh, only just,' she muttered at last, setting the mugs on the counter and turning to the fridge for milk.

'You write romantic novels, I understand,' he said, pursuing it. He grinned. 'Where do you get your inspiration?'

Well, not from men like you, thought Rachel, unsure how to answer him. 'I—er—I have a good imagination.'

'Not just that, surely?' He grinned again. 'Daisy's very proud of you.'

Rachel's smile was thin. 'Daisy's biased,' she said, wondering why she felt this need to deny her success. For heaven's sake, she was proud of her achievement. Two successful titles and her agent panting for her next manuscript—it was a would-be writer's dream.

He shrugged then, and, turning away from the bar, he walked to the windows that overlooked the garden at the back of the house. 'Nice view,' he commented, taking in the smooth stretch of lawn, the small summer-house that Steve's father had built when Daisy was a baby. 'Have you lived here long?'

Rachel's lips tightened. 'Didn't Steve tell you?'

He swung round then, hands resting low on his hips, dark eyes frankly curious. 'No,' he said flatly. 'Steve didn't tell me a lot about you. Should he have done? Am I treading on someone's toes here?'

Rachel immediately felt dreadful. 'No,' she said unhappily. 'Sorry. Don't take any notice of me. I was just being bitchy.'

Joe arched his dark brows. 'That still doesn't answer my question: what is Steve supposed to have told me?'

'Oh…' Rachel wished she'd never started this. 'It's just, well, this house used to belong to Steve's parents. They gave it to us when we got married, and…and after the divorce…' She shrugged. 'They wanted us—Daisy and me—to stay here.'

'Ah.' He seemed to understand. 'They didn't approve of the divorce?'

'Something like that.' In actual fact, Steve's parents had been outraged when the son they'd always worshipped had proved to be less than godlike.

Joe looked thoughtful. 'And were you wondering if your ex-husband had sent me here?' he asked after a moment.

It had crossed her mind, but Rachel chose not to admit it. 'I'm just wondering why you came here, Mr Mendez,' she said steadily. Then, as the coffee finished filtering, 'Black or with milk?'

'Black,' he said, as she'd guessed he would. 'And call me Joe, please. Mr Mendez sounds like my father.'

Rachel poured the coffee without answering him. But she was thinking that perhaps she had made a mistake, after all. Perhaps this man wasn't Steve's boss. Perhaps his father was.

The coffee smelt delicious and Rachel, who tended to survive on caffeine during the day, pushed a mug towards Joe Mendez and then lifted her own mug to her lips. It was hot, but so refreshing that she took a generous swallow before looking at him again. 'Shall we go back into the sitting room?'

He shrugged as if it was of little importance to him, but taking his cue from her, he followed her across the hall and into the other room. He waited until she'd seated herself in a tapestry-covered armchair before resuming his seat on the sofa, sampling his own coffee with apparent enjoyment.

'This is good,' he said, glancing round the room as he spoke. Then, his eyes finding hers again, 'I hope I'm not wasting too much of your time.'

Rachel gave a wry smile. 'My work's not that important,' she assured him. She grimaced. 'Actually, I could do with the break.'

'Not going well?'

He sounded genuinely interested and she decided to take his words at face value. 'You could say that,' she admitted. 'Since—well, since Daisy's been invited to Florida, there's been a lot to do.'

Joe regarded her intently. 'You don't want her to go?' he asked shrewdly, and Rachel couldn't prevent the faint trace of colour that entered her cheeks at his words.

'Oh, no. I mean, yes, I want her to go. She hasn't seen her father for almost a year, and it's important for them to keep in touch. It's just…'

'A big step for her to take on her own?' he suggested gently, and she was amazed at his perspicacity.

It suddenly seemed as if she'd misjudged him, and with a rueful shrug she said, 'Yes, I suppose so.' She pulled a wry face. 'I've never even crossed the Atlantic myself.'

Joe grimaced. 'It's not that big a deal. We Americans speak the same language, at least. Even if we don't always understand one another.'

Rachel smiled. 'Are you an American? I thought I detected—I don't know—a faint accent, but I could be—'

'My parents were born in Venezuela,' he interrupted her easily. 'But I've lived in the States all my life. My parents moved to Miami before I was born, and I guess I consider myself an American first and a Venezuelan second.'

Rachel nodded. Almost involuntarily, she was relaxing, and it was only when the phone rang that she realised she still didn't really know why he'd come here.

'Excuse me,' she said, getting up and going out into the hall to use the extension there. 'I won't be a minute.'

He nodded, but she was aware of him getting to his feet

and she made a point of closing the door behind her. Then, hurrying to the phone, she lifted the receiver. 'Yes?'

'Rachel?' It was her mother-in-law, and immediately she thought of Daisy.

'Yes. Is something wrong? Daisy's with you, isn't she?'

'Yes, she's here.' Evelyn Carlyle spoke affectionately. 'We've just been discussing her trip to Florida. Are you sure you're all right with this, Rachel? I mean, Steve has no right—'

'I'm fine with it,' said Rachel quickly, aware of other ears that might be listening behind the sitting room door. 'Is that why you rang, Lynnie?'

'No, no,' Evelyn was swift to reassure her. 'As a matter of fact, I was a little worried about you, dear. Madge Freeman tells me you've had a visitor this morning. She was on her way into town and she saw a strange man at your door, and I just wondered if you were all right.'

Trust Madge Freeman, thought Rachel drily, aware that the elderly lady who lived opposite missed little that went on in the Close. 'I'm okay,' she said now, playing for time. 'How have you had a conversation with Mrs Freeman? Surely she didn't ring you just to tell you I'd had a visitor?'

'Well, no…' Evelyn sounded a little put out. 'Daisy and I bumped into her at the supermarket.' She paused and then continued determinedly, 'So who was it, dear? I told Madge it was probably just one of those double-glazing salesmen.'

Rachel didn't think Joe Mendez would have appreciated being thought of as a double-glazing salesman, but she was curiously loath to discuss her visitor with her mother-in-law.

Which was silly, she told herself, but aware that her conversation might be audible to her visitor, she said, 'It's Mr Mendez. Ask Daisy. She'll tell you all about him.'

'Mendez?' Evelyn evidently recognised the name. 'Isn't that the company Steve works for?'

Rachel sighed. 'It is.'

Evelyn made a sound of impatience. 'So why is he visiting you? Nothing's happened to Steve, has it?'

'Not as far as I'm aware,' said Rachel drily, wondering why her mother-in-law would imagine that she might be informed in such circumstances. 'No, I think he's just come to reassure me that he'll look after Daisy on the flight to Florida.' She hesitated. 'I'm sure Daisy's told you all about it.'

'Well, she's said something,' replied her mother-in-law grudgingly. 'And that's the only reason he came?'

Rachel blew out a breath. 'I think so.' She knew a moment's irritation. 'That is, I'm sure so. But I've got to go, Lynnie. He'll be wondering why I'm taking so long.'

'He's still there?' Evelyn sounded shocked now, and Rachel felt almost guilty for having to admit that he was. 'But it must be over an hour since Madge saw him ringing your bell.'

And your point is? mouthed Rachel silently, copying one of Daisy's favourite expressions. But all she said was, 'I made coffee.' She managed a light laugh. 'And mine's probably cold by now.'

'Hmm.' Evelyn sniffed. 'Well, you'd better get back to your visitor, then, hadn't you? Ring me when he's gone, just so I know you're okay, right?'

Rachel shook her head. Yeah, right, she thought, but with a casual, 'Speak to you later,' she put down the receiver.

CHAPTER TWO

WHEN she re-entered the sitting room, Rachel found it was deserted. The empty mug sitting on the glass-topped coffee table in front of the hearth was the only proof she hadn't imagined her disturbing visitor. Except for Madge Freeman, of course. And that surprisingly testy call from her mother-in-law.

She caught her lower lip between her teeth as a draught of cool air alerted her to the fact that the French doors were partly open. Moving across the room, she saw Joe Mendez on the patio outside, leaning indolently against the basketball post Daisy had had her grandfather erect for her at the beginning of the summer.

As if she'd clumped across the room in hiking boots instead of her bare feet, he turned as she approached the windows. 'I hope you don't mind,' he said as he came towards her. He nodded over his shoulder. 'Who looks after the yard?'

'The yard?' Rachel's brows drew together for a moment as she backed out of his way. 'Oh, you mean the garden.' She grimaced. 'I do. When I can find the time.'

'You do a good job,' he commented, sliding the door closed behind him. 'It's nice. Colourful.'

Rachel smiled. 'That's probably all the weeds,' she said modestly. Then, 'Sorry to be so long. That was my—um—Steve's mother.'

'Ah.' He nodded. 'Mrs Carlyle.' He paused, pulling a wry face. 'Steve asked me to check on them while I was here.'

Rachel stared at him. 'But you said—'

'He didn't ask me to check on you,' Joe assured her flatly. 'That was my idea.'

'To check on me?'

'No.' Joe ran a frustrated hand around the back of his neck, his nails scraping over the stubble at his nape. 'I just wanted to meet you.' He paused, his dark brows descending. 'Not a good idea?'

'No...' Now it was Rachel's turn to look uneasy. She was intensely aware of the way his stomach had flexed when he'd raised his arm, biceps clenching, the dark outline of a tattoo just visible below his sleeve. 'It's just—'

'I guess I wanted to reassure you that your daughter will be safe with me,' he continued, his hand falling to his side again. 'My pilot's the best. Totally trustworthy, totally reliable.'

'Your pilot?' Rachel blinked, and gave a bewildered shake of her head. 'Does that mean you're not using commercial transport?'

'Didn't Steve tell you?'

As a matter of fact, Steve hadn't told her anything, Rachel reflected flatly. The invitation had come in one of his occasional emails to his daughter, and she'd just naturally assumed...

She attempted to regroup. 'Does Daisy know this?' she asked, wondering if Daisy had received another message she knew nothing about.

It wasn't a pleasant thought. She and Daisy had a pretty good relationship, all things considered, and, apart from the usual gripes about homework and curfews, she'd have said her daughter never kept anything from her.

Joe shrugged. 'I guess so,' he said, evidently aware of her disapproval. 'Hey, it's not a big deal. You can come check out the plane for yourself, if you like.'

Rachel gazed at him incredulously. 'And that would achieve what, exactly?' she asked, aware that her voice had risen several notches. 'I think you'd better go, Mr Mendez. I need to speak to Daisy. If—if you have a number where I can reach you afterwards...'

Joe regarded her closely, those intense dark eyes bringing a surge of colour to her cheeks. 'Don't you trust me?' he asked, and Rachel sucked in a disbelieving breath.

'I don't know you, Mr Mendez. I don't know whether I can trust you or not. I just need to think about what you've told me.'

Joe shook his head. 'Okay.' There was a faint trace of hostility in his tone now, and Rachel prayed she wasn't treading on anyone's toes here. Even Steve's, she added reluctantly, though why the hell he hadn't told her what was going on she didn't know.

'So, if I can get back to you...' she ventured unhappily, and then jerked back in alarm when he reached for his jacket lying on the arm of the sofa beside her. For a crazy moment, she'd thought he was reaching for her, and a trace of the panic she'd momentarily felt showed in her face.

But she should have had more sense, she chided herself as he picked up the jacket and searched his inside pocket for a card and a pen. A man like Joe Mendez would have no trouble in finding a woman if he wanted one. He'd scarcely waste his time and energies on a thirty-something divorcée with very ordinary features and dirty-blonde hair.

Linking her fingers tightly together at her waist, she prayed he hadn't noticed her mistake. For heaven's sake, what was the matter with her? It wasn't as if she hadn't dated anyone since Steve had walked out on her. Okay, she'd only slept with one man, but she should still have remembered the difference between civility and sex.

Meanwhile, Joe was scribbling something on the back of a business card, and after a moment he handed it over. 'This proves who I am, and I've given you my present address,' he said somewhat drily. 'I've written my cell number, too. Call me when you've decided what you want to do.'

'Thanks.'

Rachel took the card with nervous fingers, unable to deny the jolt of electricity she felt when his hand touched hers. Her eyes darted to his, but she had no idea if he'd been aware of it. There was a guarded quality about his gaze now, and thick black lashes any woman would have envied swept down to obscure his expression.

'No problem,' he said, hooking his jacket over one shoulder and heading towards the open door. He swung open the outer door and then paused on the threshold. 'Tell Daisy I said hi,' he added tightly before starting down the path to the gate.

Ridiculously, Rachel felt guilty the minute she'd closed the door. She felt as if she'd totally screwed up, and she could imagine how Daisy would react when she told her what had happened. But for goodness' sake, Mendez was a stranger. To her, at least, she amended with an impatient click of her tongue. Just because Daisy had met him before didn't mean *she* had to trust him.

But it was neither his trustworthiness nor Daisy's probable frustration that accompanied her into the kitchen when she went to rinse out their coffee mugs. It was the effect he had had—was still having, if she was honest—on her. Damn it, the hairs on her neck still prickled when she thought about him. And she could remember every detail about him with a meticulousness that bordered on the extreme.

The sound of the phone ringing was a welcome relief, though she suspected she knew who her caller was. And she was right. 'Rachel? I thought you were going to ring me when your visitor had gone.'

'How do you know he has gone?' muttered Rachel to herself, feeling grumpy, but she managed to adopt a reasonable tone. 'He's just left,' she said brightly. 'Um—can I speak to Daisy?'

'No.' Her mother-in-law didn't sound very pleased. 'That was why I was ringing, actually. She's on her way home. As soon as she heard Mr Mendez was there she insisted on taking off. She's going to be very disappointed when she gets home and finds he's not there.'

I'll bet, thought Rachel drily, and not just because of that. 'Okay,' she responded. 'I expect she'll give you a ring later.'

'Hmph.' Evelyn Carlyle snorted. 'Well, remind her to do it, will you? We always like to know she's safely home.'

'I will.'

Rachel couldn't believe she was getting off so lightly, but just as she was about to put down the receiver, Evelyn spoke again. 'So—what did you think of him? Had he only come to reassure you about Daisy's trip? He lives in Florida, doesn't he? It's good of him to offer to escort her, don't you think?'

Rachel pressed her lips together. But only briefly. 'Very good,' she managed, not prepared to get into the details with Evelyn right now. To her relief, she heard a key being inserted in the front door. 'Oh, this sounds like Daisy now. Speak to you later.'

This time she put the receiver down before Evelyn could say anything else and stood, feeling ridiculously apprehensive as Daisy let herself into the house. The girl looked round expectantly, and then, when her mother didn't say anything, she exclaimed, 'Don't tell me he's gone!'

'Afraid so.' Rachel forced a smile and walked back into the kitchen. The two coffee mugs on the drainer seemed to reproach her, and Daisy, following her, gave an indignant cry.

'You gave him coffee?'

Rachel busied herself with tidying the counter. 'Shouldn't I have done?' she asked lightly. 'I always offer visitors coffee, you know that.'

'So why isn't he still here? Grandma only rang about twenty minutes ago.'

'I know.'

'So what? Didn't he like the coffee?'

Rachel sighed and said carefully, 'We'd already had a conversation before your grandmother phoned. You must know that, too. You were at the supermarket when you met Mrs Freeman, weren't you?'

'Yes.' Daisy sounded sulky now.

'Well, then.'

'What I don't understand is why you didn't ring me and tell me he was here.' Daisy scowled. 'You knew I'd like to meet him again.' She shrugged. 'Oh, well, I suppose we'll have plenty of time to talk on the flight.'

She turned away, but now Rachel felt a twinge of impatience. 'Oh, yes,' she said tightly. 'On the flight to Florida. In his *private* plane.'

If she'd had any doubts that Daisy knew what she was talking about they'd have been extinguished at that moment. Her daughter's face suffused with colour, and she couldn't have looked any more guilty if she'd tried.

'He told you,' she said lamely, and Rachel felt a disappointed hollowing in her stomach.

'Unlike you,' she said, regarding Daisy with cool eyes. 'I assume your father informed you of the arrangement?'

'Well, yes.' Daisy hunched her shoulders, looking suddenly much younger than her years. 'I'm sorry, Mum.'

Rachel shook her head. 'And…what? You decided to keep it to yourself?'

'Dad said you probably wouldn't understand.' She hesitated. 'He said there was no need for you to know.'

'Oh, Daisy!'

'I know.' Daisy bit into her lower lip. 'But, well, I didn't think it was that important.'

'So why didn't you tell me anyway?'

Daisy shrugged.

'Because you knew how I'd react,' Rachel answered for her. 'Really, Daisy, I thought we were always honest with one another.'

'We are.'

'Except when your father asks you not to be, apparently,' declared Rachel tersely, aware she was breaking her own rules about not slagging off Steve to his daughter. 'Oh, well, it's done now. But I have to tell you, it's something I need to think about and I've told Mr Mendez the same.'

Daisy gasped now. 'You mean you've implied you might not agree to my going with him?'

Rachel refused to feel cowed. 'I've said I'll ring him after I've spoken with you.' She paused, and then added defensively, 'What did you expect me to say, Daisy? That I've got no objections to you flying for—what?—twelve hours in a plane with a man I hardly know?'

'Daddy says it's about nine hours, actually.'

'Well *nine* hours, then.' Rachel felt angry again. 'Oh, yes, your father knew what he was doing when he asked you not to tell me what was going on.'

Daisy's lips pursed. 'It's not like Mr Mendez is a—a pervert or something.'

'All right. I'll admit he seems respectable enough…'

'Respectable!' Daisy scoffed.

'But I should have been given the full story, not just your father's edited version.'

'I know.' Daisy sighed. 'I tried to tell him that. Like, in my emails. But you know what he's like.'

Not any more, mused Rachel, aware of a surprising wave of relief at the thought. Suddenly the memory of her ex-husband seemed distant and indistinct, usurped by the image of a man whose raw sexuality had assaulted her senses in a way Steve never had.

Not wanting Daisy to detect what she was thinking and attribute any of it to her father, Rachel drew a deep breath and opened the door of the fridge. 'Anyway,' she said, 'I've said I'll think about it, and I will. Now, what would you like for lunch? I have to warn you, I expected you to have lunch at Grandma's, so I don't have anything special to offer you.'

Daisy seemed anxious now. But not about her lunch. 'You're not thinking of changing your mind, are you, Mum?' she asked, and Rachel wondered how sincere her daughter's offer not to go to Florida had really been. 'I mean, you liked him, didn't you?'

'Who?'

'Mr Mendez.'

Rachel shrugged. 'He seemed very nice.' And how insincere was that? 'But that has nothing to do with it.'

Daisy was looking really worried, and despite her resentment towards Steve for putting her in this situation, Rachel felt a reluctant surge of sympathy for her. She was only thirteen, after all, and she didn't deserve to suffer because of their marital politics.

'Just leave it for now,' she said, taking a carton of eggs out of the fridge to avoid looking at her daughter. 'How about pancakes? Or would you prefer take-out?'

The subject was dropped but not forgotten. It was only four days until Daisy was due to leave for Florida, and Rachel knew she couldn't delay indefinitely.

After lunch, Daisy disappeared up to her room and Rachel wondered if she was emailing her father with the latest developments. She spent the afternoon expecting an irate email from her ex-husband, but when she checked her mail before closing the computer there were only two messages: one from a friend in London and the other from her agent.

Supper was not a comfortable meal. Rachel opened a bottle of red wine that she'd been saving for a special occasion—but with Daisy only pushing her pasta round her plate, giving her mother soulful looks every time their eyes met, the effort was wasted.

Eventually, after blocking every opening her mother tried to make, Daisy said, 'How's your book going?' and Rachel was so taken aback she could hardly think of a response. Daisy had never shown any interest in her writing before, regarding it in much the same light as any child regarded a parent's occupation.

'Um—it's going okay,' she said at last, getting up to pour herself another glass of Merlot. 'I expect I'll get it finished while you're away.'

'So I am going, then?' Daisy pounced on the admission.

'I expect so.' Rachel wished she hadn't brought the subject up again.

'Oh, good.' Daisy leant forward and attacked her plate with renewed enthusiasm. 'I knew you wouldn't really stop me from going.'

Rachel shook her head, but she didn't deny it. How could she? But she did intend to speak to her ex-husband about the arrangements as soon as Daisy was asleep.

She managed to catch Steve before he went out for the evening. He was predictably miffed at receiving a call from his ex-wife at home. Any communication between them—infrequent though it was—was usually conducted during office hours, and he was even more annoyed when he heard why Rachel wanted to speak to him.

'Oh, for pity's sake, Rache!' he exclaimed, using the abbreviation of her name that she'd never liked. 'What's your problem? I'd have thought you'd be pleased she wasn't having to travel in an economy seat. Besides, Mendez is a great guy. I don't know what kind of creeps you've been dating since you and I split, but take my word for it, you've got nothing to worry about from him.'

Rachel took a deep breath, pressing her lips together for a moment to prevent the angry retort she wanted to make. Then she said stiffly, 'Very well. But I wish you'd contacted me before making different arrangements.'

'Yeah, right.' Steve was sardonic. 'Why do you think I—?' He broke off and another feminine voice could be heard in the background. 'I know, I know. I'm coming, baby,' he said in an aside, and then, his tone sharpening, 'So, when Mendez gets in touch with you, you won't put up any objections, right?'

'When he…?' Rachel licked her lips. 'Well, as a matter of fact, he's already been in touch.'

'He has?' Steve was wary.

'Yes.' Rachel hesitated. 'He came to the house today.'

Steve swore to himself, and once again Rachel heard that other voice, which must have been Lauren's, making some kind of protest. 'Yeah, yeah, I'm coming,' he said again, his tone much less indulgent now. There was another brief exchange and then he addressed himself to Rachel again. 'Don't tell me you let Mendez know how you felt? Damn it, Rache, the man owns the company!'

Rachel stifled a groan. Until that moment, she'd been assuring herself that it had to be Joe Mendez's father who was the real power behind Mendez Macrosystems, but now she was forced to revise her opinion.

'I—I may have done,' she allowed in a low voice, and Steve swore again.

'Are you completely crazy?' he demanded angrily. 'For God's sake, Rachel, do you want me to lose my job? Is that what this is all about?'

Rachel had been feeling rather guilty for creating a difficult situation, but Steve's attitude really ticked her off. 'You have to be joking,' she retorted coldly. 'Why would I want to run the risk of forcing you to return to England? Believe me, Steve, I have no desire to see your lying face again.'

She'd slammed down the receiver and was standing, staring at the phone, when she heard a stair creak behind her. She turned in time to see Daisy, dressed only in the vest and shorts she used to sleep in, creeping cautiously back up the stairs. She'd obviously heard at least the end of what her mother had said, and her cheeks turned pink with embarrassment when Rachel spoke her name.

'I'm sorry,' she muttered, looking shamefaced. 'I didn't realise it was Dad you were talking to. I—I thought something might have happened to Granddad or Grandma.'

Rachel doubted that, but she wasn't in the mood to start another argument. Not tonight. 'It's okay,' she said. 'I just wanted to speak to your father about the arrangements. Go on back to bed. There's nothing for you to worry about. I'll be up myself in a few minutes.'

Daisy hesitated. 'You and Dad are never likely to get back together, are you?' she murmured regretfully, and Rachel thought how depressing it was when a child was involved.

'No,' she said gently. 'I'm sorry, sweetheart. It's just not going to happen.'

'Oh, well.' Daisy shrugged. 'I guess I can live with it. I mean, you're bound to meet someone else someday. Someone really nice. Not like Lauren at all.'

It was after midnight when Rachel tumbled into bed, but for once she didn't immediately fall asleep. Usually her eyes were so tired she lost consciousness the minute her head touched the pillow, but tonight her mind was too active to relax.

It was ringing Steve so late, she decided. With the time lag, she'd had to wait until after eleven to catch him at home. But it hadn't been something she'd wanted to discuss while he was at the office, even on his mobile phone, with possibly a receptionist or a secretary listening in.

However, it wasn't Steve's image that kept her awake until the early hours. It wasn't his blond good looks and slim athleticism that haunted her sleep. The image she found behind her eyes was that of Joe Mendez, whose tough, somewhat ruthless features and muscled profile ticked every one of the boxes Daisy might have desired…

CHAPTER THREE

THERE was someone at the door. Rachel could hear the bell ringing quite clearly and she struggled up in bed, wondering who on earth would call at this hour of the morning.

But it wasn't the doorbell. As soon as she sat up and got her bearings, she realised it was the phone beside the bed that had awakened her. It was silent now. Daisy must have answered it downstairs, she thought resignedly. It wasn't like her daughter to be up so early, but it was holiday time, not a school morning; go figure.

What time was it? she wondered, groping for the small travelling clock she kept beside the bed. She was horrified when she saw it was after ten o'clock. She rarely slept in, but after the restless night she'd had it was hardly surprising. She must have fallen asleep eventually, but right now she felt decidedly rough.

Pushing her legs out of bed, she swayed a little as she got to her feet. Too much red wine, she thought, hauling on her towelling bathrobe and opening the bedroom door. Wasn't it just typical that, the one morning someone chose to call her this early, she was still in bed?

She almost jumped out of her skin when the phone began to ring again. She'd stepped out onto the landing, wondering where Daisy had got to, when its insistent peal assaulted her ears. Daisy could answer it, she thought, starting down the stairs. It was most likely someone for her.

But Daisy didn't answer it and Rachel looked back up the stairs, wondering if her daughter had slept in too. Daisy's bedroom door was closed, but that didn't prove anything. She tended to regard her bedroom as her private space, and Rachel rarely intruded without an invitation.

Continuing down the stairs, Rachel picked up the receiver in the hall. 'Yes?' she said, the headache that was beginning to throb behind her temples making her sound snappy.

'Rachel?' Her throat dried. Oh God, it was him again. Joe Mendez. He must be ringing to find out what she'd decided. Had he spoken to Steve? 'I just wanted—'

'To know about Daisy,' she interrupted him quickly. 'I did intend to ring you later today.'

'No.' Joe spoke crisply. 'I didn't ring you to find out about Daisy. I know you've agreed to let her go. She told me so herself.'

Rachel blinked. 'She *told* you?' She was confused.

'Wait a second.' There was a momentary shifting of the phone, a muffled protest, and then a reluctant voice said, 'Hello, Mum.'

It was Daisy. Rachel groped for the oak chest that served as both a place to drop the mail and somewhere to sit to change one's shoes and sank down onto it. 'Daisy!' Her voice cracked. 'What's going on?'

'Don't be mad, Mum.' Daisy, at least, knew how she was feeling. 'I had to come and see Mr Mendez. I had to tell him you were okay with me travelling with him.'

Rachel felt dazed. 'Why?'

'Well, because I heard what you said to Dad, and I didn't—'

'Anything I said to your father was between us two, do you understand that?' Rachel's headache felt so much worse now. 'Honestly, Daisy, I thought I could trust you. Now—now I don't know what to think.'

'Oh, Mum.'

'Where are you, anyway?'

'At—at Mr Mendez's house.'

'His house?' Rachel was stunned. 'How did you know where he was staying?'

'It was on his card,' muttered Daisy unhappily. 'You just left it in the hall, and I—I picked it up.'

'Oh, Daisy!' Rachel could hardly take it in. 'You had no right to read that card, let alone go out without my permission to visit someone you hardly know!'

'Don't be like that, Mum, please.'

'How do you expect me to be?' Rachel felt her temper rising. 'I can't believe you'd do something so deceitful. Particularly as I've been awake half the night worrying about this trip.' Well, that was only partly true, but Daisy didn't need to know that. 'And now I discover you've taken matters into your own hands.'

There was another muffled exchange and then Joe said, 'Sorry if this has been a bit of a shock. I guess you've been wondering where Daisy was. I'm going to bring her home, but I felt I ought to let you know she's okay.'

Rachel's shoulders hunched. She was too ashamed to say she hadn't even known her daughter had gone out, but she managed a polite, 'That was kind of you.'

'Yeah, well.' She suspected he might have detected the irony in her voice and his next words seemed to prove it. 'Don't be too hard on her, right? I think she meant well.'

Rachel tried not to feel resentful that this man—this stranger—felt he had the right to advise her about how to treat her daughter. But all she said was, 'Thanks. I appreciate your comments,' and rang off before indignation got the better of politeness.

However, as soon as she'd replaced the receiver she realised she had no idea where Joe's—house? Hotel?—was. She'd hardly glanced at his card. And now she could only guess how much time she might have before they got here.

She was desperate for a cup of coffee, but she didn't dare wait while it brewed. Instead, she spooned grains into the filter and left it to percolate while she took a swift shower.

Her hair was still damp when she stood in front of the mirror in her bedroom, surveying her appearance. Tucking the artificially darkened strands back behind her ears, she decided it didn't look too bad. It was foolish, she knew, but instead of her usual working gear of shorts and a cotton top she'd chosen to wear a dress. It was a simple camisole, in shades of cream and brown, which she thought complemented her lightly tanned skin. The dress ended at her knees, and she left her legs bare.

The shower had eased her headache somewhat, but she took two paracetamol with her coffee. Then, realising she hadn't put on any make-up, she dashed back upstairs, and was in the process of brushing a bronze shadow onto her lids when she heard a car in the road outside.

Her hand shook for a moment, and she was forced to repair the damage before realising she hadn't time to put on any lipstick now. She could hear Daisy opening the door downstairs and, praying she didn't look as nervous as she felt, Rachel smoothed damp palms over her hips and left the room.

Descending the stairs, she felt as if she'd timed her entrance. Which simply wasn't true. She would have much preferred to be drinking her coffee in the kitchen when they arrived, and she hoped Joe didn't think it was deliberate.

Still, she couldn't prevent her eyes from sliding over him before they fastened on her daughter. He was more formally dressed this morning, his charcoal-grey suit and lighter grey shirt fairly screaming their designer label. His only concession to the occasion was the fact that he wasn't wearing a tie. The top two buttons of his shirt weren't fastened and, as she came down the stairs, she was offered a disturbing glimpse of night-dark hair in the opening.

Predictably, it was Daisy who spoke first. 'You look nice, Mum,' she said, and Rachel felt an embarrassing wave of colour surge into her face. Not that she didn't know what Daisy was trying to do. Her daughter wasn't exactly subtle.

But Joe was watching and, although her eyes promised retribution later on, she said, 'Thank you.' Then, more pointedly, 'You should have let me know you were going out.'

'I didn't want to wake you,' said Daisy blithely, and Rachel hoped that Joe didn't think she often overslept.

'How thoughtful,' she managed, before turning to their visitor. 'I'm sorry about this, Mr Mendez. I had no idea Daisy would come to your house.'

'No problem.' His dark eyes were disturbingly intent as they rested on her hot face, and Rachel felt as if her insides had turned to liquid. 'She's quite a character, your daughter.' His mouth twisted. 'And very entertaining.'

'Is she?' Rachel wondered what Daisy had been saying to inspire that kind of response.

But before she could say anything else he spoke again. 'Well, I guess I better get going. I've got a lunch meeting with some business colleagues at twelve o'clock.'

Rachel licked her lips. 'You wouldn't like some coffee before you leave?' she ventured, and then chided herself anew when he shook his head.

'Not right now, thanks,' he said, pulling a face at Daisy when she showed her disappointment. His gaze switched back to Rachel. 'How would it be if I called you later about the arrangements for Monday? I've got your number, if you'll forgive the pun.'

Rachel nodded. 'This afternoon, you mean?'

'Or this evening?' He gave her a quizzical look. 'Will you be in?'

Most definitely, thought Rachel ruefully, but she managed to sound as if she'd had to think about it. 'I'll be here,' she agreed.

'Great.' A trace of a smile appeared. 'Speak to you later then.'

As she watched him walk down the path to the gate, Rachel wondered what had ever possessed her to think that he'd want to spend any more time with her than he had to. He'd done the gentlemanly thing and brought Daisy home, but that was that. Job done.

She closed the door without waiting for him to get into his car. After Monday, she'd probably never see him again. And that was just as well for all concerned. Now all she had to do was deal with Daisy who, she noticed wryly, had already made herself scarce….

Joe drove back to his house in Eaton Court Mews with an odd sense of frustration. He felt as if he'd handled the whole business with Rachel Carlyle badly. But, damn it, he was doing her a favour here, wasn't he? So why the hell did he feel as if he was in the wrong?

He scowled. He wished he'd never offered to give the kid a ride across the Atlantic now. It was creating all sorts of problems he hadn't even thought of when Steve had told him his daughter was coming to Florida for a visit.

In truth, he'd felt sorry for the guy. It couldn't be easy, living the better part of four-thousand miles from your only offspring, and according to Steve his ex-wife had blocked his last few attempts to see Daisy. Naturally she could only come to stay during her school vacations, but at both Christmas and Easter Rachel had had other plans.

That was why he'd suggested that the kid could travel with him. Surely her mother could have no objections to that? He and Steve had known one another for over five years, ever since Carlyle had come to work for Mendez Macrosystems in London, and since his move to Miami last year they'd become friends.

But evidently Steve hadn't chosen to tell his ex-wife of the arrangements. Despite what he'd been told about her, Joe didn't think Rachel's shock at learning that Daisy wouldn't be flying on a commercial airline was simulated. She hadn't known. He'd bet his life on it.

He shook his head. Which begged the question: why hadn't Steve told her? Okay, he was prepared to accept that their relationship must have suffered when they'd got a divorce, but she could hardly blame Steve for that. According to the account he'd heard, there'd been faults on both sides, not least the fact that Rachel had done everything she could to sabotage her husband's career. Ted Johansen had told him that Lauren would never have got involved with Steve if he and Rachel hadn't been having problems. According to him, his daughter wasn't that kind of girl.

Something Joe had reserved judgment about.

Nevertheless, Steve should have explained what was happening. Just because he found Rachel difficult to reason with didn't excuse him entirely, and Joe had every intention of giving him a piece of his mind when he got back to the States.

Now he pulled the Lexus into Eaton Court Mews and drew up outside the house he'd bought on one of his frequent trips to London. He'd liked it because of its character and antiquity, its wisteria-clad walls a far cry from the busy thoroughfare that passed just a few feet beyond the arched entrance to the mews.

He entered via an oak-studded door to one side of the ground-floor garage and took the stairs to the next floor, where the first level of living rooms was situated. It had taken him some time to get used to not calling this the 'second floor', as they did back home, but Charles Barry, his English housekeeper, was gradually educating him.

Charles himself appeared as Joe walked into a comfortably furnished sitting room. Furniture, which Charles had helped him choose, gave the room an attractive authenticity, with lots of polished wood and distressed-leather sofas beneath the narrow-paned dormer windows.

'Mission accomplished?' he asked, referring to his employer's undertaking to deliver Daisy back to her mother, and Joe pulled an amused face.

'I guess so,' he said, without conviction. He shook his head. 'I just wish I didn't have the feeling that I'm the bad guy here.'

Charles, a slim, prematurely grey-haired man in his fifties, arched an enquiring brow. 'Mrs Carlyle doesn't appreciate your consideration, I gather?'

'You could say that.'

'Something of a harridan, is she?'

'Hell, no.' The words were out before Joe could stop them. But they were true. No way could Rachel Carlyle be described as a harridan. And that was possibly one of the reasons why he was feeling so frustrated now.

Charles frowned. 'I detect a note of ambiguity here,' he said. 'Do I take it you're having second thoughts about delivering the girl to her father?'

Joe's jaw compressed. 'Steve didn't bother to tell his ex-wife that Daisy would be travelling with me,' he explained flatly. 'On the Jetstream, I mean. She assumed we'd be using public transport.'

'I see.' Charles considered this. 'And that's created a problem?'

Joe gave a curt nod. 'You got it.'

'Ah.' Charles was thoughtful. 'But surely, now that she's met you for herself, Mrs Carlyle must be reassured?'

'You think?'

'She's not?' Charles looked taken aback. 'So what kind of woman is she? Didn't Mr Carlyle say that she's a writer?' He cupped his chin in one hand. 'I'm imagining a rather…overweight lady, all flowing scarves and Birkenstocks. Am I right?'

Joe couldn't prevent the laugh that erupted from him then.

'You couldn't be more wrong!' he exclaimed, picturing Rachel as he'd first seen her in her cotton vest and shorts. 'No, she's not overweight, Charles. She's not skinny, you understand? She's got some shape. But she's not fat.'

Charles regarded him intently. 'But not young? Not like the second Mrs Carlyle?'

'No.' Joe conceded the point. Steve had definitely gone for looks over intelligence the second time around. It had also helped that Lauren's old man was one of the directors of the company, he reflected, before adding, 'But Rachel's okay. Quite attractive, actually.'

Charles' brows ascended again. 'Well…' He didn't appear to know how to answer that so, changing the subject, he asked if his employer would like something to drink before he left for his meeting. 'You did say you had a luncheon appointment,' he reminded him politely, and Joe glanced somewhat impatiently at his watch.

'Oh, yeah,' He blew out a breath. Then, 'No, that's okay.' He nodded towards the built-in bar hidden behind a wall of bookshelves. 'I'll get myself a soda, if I want one.'

'Yes, sir.'

Charles withdrew and Joe moved across to the windows, staring out unseeingly onto the mews below. He found himself wondering what exactly had gone wrong with the Carlyles' marriage. Sure, he'd heard Steve's—and Johansen's—interpretation of events. But having met Rachel personally, he found it harder to believe that she would neglect her home and family in favour of her career. A woman like that would hardly put up any opposition to exactly how her daughter was to travel to Florida. Indeed, she'd probably be glad of the break from teenage angst, however it was going to be achieved.

Still, he had to factor in the probable resistance she had to Daisy spending any time with her father and stepmother. If Steve was to be believed—and until the last couple of days he'd had no reason to doubt that he was—she'd done her best to turn Daisy against him and Lauren.

His scowl returned. He could so do without this, he thought irritably. Do without this damned lunch with the company's British executives, too. If he hadn't promised his father to follow in his footsteps, and keep all branches of Macrosystems in the frame, he'd have scrubbed any and all business meetings and spent the rest of the day at the nearest race track.

Still, this evening he had his date with Shelley Adair to look forward to. She'd been most put out when he'd cried off the party she'd been giving the evening before. But after his altercation with Rachel Carlyle, he hadn't been in the mood for the kind of noisy reception Shelley favoured. Besides, if he was perfectly honest, he'd expected Rachel to have second thoughts and ring him to apologise and, when she hadn't, he'd gone to bed feeling decidedly aggrieved.

So why was he wasting more time thinking about her? He'd been downright astounded when Daisy had turned up at his door this morning. It had been the last thing he'd expected, and at first he'd thought she'd come because her mother had asked her to. Finding out Rachel hadn't even known she'd left the house had soon disabused him of that notion, and he'd been half inclined to blame Daisy's behaviour on her mother. But bringing up a teenager like Daisy on her own couldn't be easy. That was why he'd reined in his own irritation when Rachel had reacted as she had.

He sighed. Were Steve's complaints about her justified? The way Rachel was acting made him inclined to think again. He just wished he wasn't involved in the situation, wished he didn't have these suspicions that she was the victim here.

CHAPTER FOUR

ON SATURDAY morning Rachel was sitting at the kitchen table, drinking her third cup of coffee of the day and trying to make sense of the pages she'd written the night before, when Daisy came clattering down the stairs.

It was barely seven, and on any normal weekend morning it would have been virtually impossible to get her daughter out of bed before nine o'clock. But clearly Daisy's mind was fixated on the same issue that had kept Rachel awake half the night.

'Did he ring?'

Daisy didn't waste time on polite preamble, and Rachel put down her coffee cup and shuffled her pages into a single pile. 'No.'

'He didn't?' Daisy stared at her aghast. 'I thought that must be why you were up so early.'

'Well, I'm sorry to disappoint you, but no one's rung. Either last night, or this morning.'

Daisy looked dismayed. 'But he said he would ring,' she protested, and Rachel thought that, despite all her efforts to appear grown up, her daughter was still very much a child with a child's simplistic view of the world.

Getting to her feet, she gave Daisy a hug and said, 'I shouldn't worry about it, sweetheart. I expect his meeting went on longer than he'd anticipated, and perhaps he had other plans for the evening.'

Plans that had no doubt included the company of some ravishing female, Rachel reflected drily. A man like Mendez was hardly likely to spend his nights alone. He was far too attractive; far too sexy. He didn't wear a wedding ring—not that that meant a lot, if Steve was anything to go by—but there was bound to be some glamorous socialite who found his slightly cruel good looks and sensual appeal absolutely fascinating. As she did, Rachel admitted reluctantly. Though in her case, she assured herself, it was a purely professional assessment.

'How long does a phone call take?' Daisy pulled away from her mother and went to take a carton of milk out of the fridge. Pouring herself a glass, she added sulkily, 'I wish Dad had arranged for me to fly with British Airways. Then we wouldn't have to rely on anyone else.'

Rachel was tempted to second that, but she was sensible enough to know that, however tardy he might be, they hadn't heard the last of Joe Mendez. 'Give it until lunchtime,' she said. 'Then, if we still haven't heard anything, I'll ring him.' She felt a hollowing in her stomach at the thought but she ignored it. 'Okay?'

'Oh, cool!' Daisy's upper lip was still coated with milk as she came and gave her mother a wet kiss on her cheek. Her delight was unmistakeable. 'Thanks, Mum.'

'You're welcome.' Refusing to consider what she was going to say if she had to contact Mendez, Rachel scrubbed the place Daisy's lips had touched with a rueful hand. Then, wrapping her cotton dressing-gown closer about her, she picked up the manuscript and started for the door. 'I'm going to have a shower,' she said. 'I won't be long. Then I'll get breakfast.'

'I can do that.' Daisy finished her milk and popped the glass into the dishwasher. 'What would you like? I can make French toast.'

'Just toast will do,' said Rachel, guessing the girl was only trying to be helpful. But as she started up the stairs she hoped that, by offering to ring Mendez, she hadn't given Daisy the idea that she wouldn't object if her daughter rang him herself.

Knowing she had to go out sometime today to do some food shopping, Rachel dressed in jeans and a black V-necked tee shirt. She dried her hair and then caught it up in a loose knot on top of her head. She didn't bother with any make-up, and a pair of strappy leather sandals completed her outfit. She looked what she was, she thought, surveying her appearance without conceit: a single mother approaching middle age, with no particular claim to either youth or beauty.

Daisy had the toast ready when she re-entered the kitchen, and there was fresh coffee simmering on the hob. Daisy had taken the time to dress too, though her baggy cut-offs and cropped tank top looked as if they'd spent the night on her bedroom floor.

'There you go,' she said, setting the toast on the table where a jar of marmalade and the butter dish already resided; if her cheeks looked a little pink, Rachel put it down to the heat of the grill.

'This looks good.' Although she wasn't feeling particularly hungry, Rachel buttered a slice of toast and spooned on a little of the marmalade. Then, taking a bite, she looked expectantly up at her daughter. 'Aren't you having any?'

'I had some cornflakes,' said Daisy quickly. 'I thought you wouldn't mind.'

'No.' But Rachel's brows drew together as she spoke. Then, dismissing the suspicion that Daisy wasn't being altogether truthful, she added, 'I'll have to go out later. We've got nothing in the fridge, and I need some fresh bread.'

'But you can't.'

Daisy spoke impulsively and Rachel looked at her with narrowed eyes. 'Why not?'

'Well—because Mr Mendez is going to phone, isn't he?'

'So?' Rachel's gaze turned to one of enquiry. 'We have an answerphone. If we're not here, I'm sure he'll leave a message, and I can ring him back.'

Daisy pressed her lips together. 'But what if he comes round?'

'Comes round?' Rachel was wary. 'Why on earth would he come round?' Not to see her, she was sure. 'He's said he'll phone. And, if he doesn't, I've already said I'll phone him.'

'He's not in,' said Daisy quickly, and Rachel's eyes widened in disbelief.

'He's not in?' she echoed. Then, shaking her head to clear it, she went on, 'How do you know he's not in?'

But she didn't need the girl to answer. She already knew. Daisy had done what she'd been half-afraid she might and had phoned Mendez while she was in the shower.

'I—I spoke to that man who works for him,' Daisy confessed unhappily. 'Mr Mendez calls him Charles.' She bit her lip, perhaps hoping that Rachel would take pity on her. But when it became apparent that her mother wasn't about to speak, she hurried on, 'He—he was really offhand.'

Rachel regarded her disapprovingly. 'And that surprises you?' She shook her head. 'It's barely eight o'clock, Daisy. It's Saturday, and people don't appreciate being woken up so early.'

Daisy's expression lightened. 'So maybe Mr Mendez was really there?' she suggested. 'But this man—Charles—didn't want to disturb him.' She looked encouragingly at her mother. 'Do you think that's what happened?'

'It's possible.' But Rachel suspected it wasn't that simple. It was far more likely that Mendez had slept elsewhere, and her stomach tightened at the thought. Then, dismissing the images that evoked from her mind, she said, 'It would serve you right if Mr Mendez decided that taking you to Florida was more trouble than it was worth. Then your father would be stuck with your air fare. I wonder how he'd feel about that?'

It was a low blow, and Rachel regretted letting her own disappointment rule her tongue. She wanted Daisy to spend time with Steve; of course she did. It was just hard to accept that her daughter wasn't so different from her father after all.

Daisy looked positively mortified now, and, knowing she couldn't let her shoulder all the blame for the way she was feeling, she sighed. 'Look, I'm sure that's not going to happen. But you have to be patient. I imagine Mr Mendez has more important matters than arranging your trip to attend to. If you take my advice, you'll let him get back to you in his own good time.'

'But what if he forgets?'

Rachel's laugh was bitter. 'Oh, I don't think that's likely,' she said drily. 'Now, I suggest you let me finish my coffee, and then you can come with me to the supermarket.'

It was after eleven by the time they got back to the house. Despite Daisy's agitation, Rachel had been determined not to let Joe Mendez think that she, at least, was desperate for his assistance. Daisy was thirteen, after all, and there was no reason why she shouldn't make the journey on her own on a commercial flight. Rachel knew that the air crew could be relied upon to keep an eye on her, and Steve would be meeting her in Miami.

Consequently, it was something of a blow to find the powerful SUV parked at their gate when she turned into Castle Close. Although she'd only seen the vehicle once before, the identity of its owner was unquestionable, and she didn't need Daisy's cry of excitement to reinforce her opinion.

'It's Mr Mendez!' Daisy exclaimed, hopping out of Rachel's modest Audi as soon as she applied the brake. 'I wonder how long he's been waiting? I told you we shouldn't have gone out.'

Rachel reserved judgment on that, but in any case she had

no time to reply. Daisy was already running to the front of the Lexus, full of excitement as she waited for Joe Mendez to open the door.

He did so at once. Long, powerful legs encased in tight-fitting black jeans again this morning appeared; tan-coloured deck shoes, once more without socks, lowered to the pavement. As she stood, Rachel glimpsed a white tee shirt in the open V of a black knitted polo, which exposed his arms and the dark shadow of his tattoo. There was a dark shadow on his jawline too, she noticed, so evidently he hadn't bothered to shave. But the slightly dishevelled look suited him. He was that kind of man.

It was an effort for her to get out of the car, but eventually she did so, aware that Daisy was chattering away happily. Probably blaming her mother for them not having been at home, thought Rachel ruefully. Well, it had been her fault, but she wasn't ashamed of it. If Daisy hadn't taken it into her head to ring the man, he'd have contacted her sooner or later. Or not—as he chose.

Meanwhile Joe was wishing Daisy would stop talking long enough to allow him to speak to her mother. Judging by the reluctance with which Rachel had got out of the vehicle, she wasn't exactly thrilled to see him. But when she opened the boot and started unloading bags of groceries onto the path, he had the perfect excuse to go and assist her.

'Hi,' he said as he reached the pile of plastic carriers. 'Let me help you.'

'I can manage.' Rachel knew she sounded ungrateful, but she couldn't help it.

However, Joe ignored her. Hefting two bags in each hand, he nodded towards the house. 'You go ahead and open the door. I'll follow you.'

Rachel's lips tightened, but short of forcibly wresting the carriers from him, she had no choice but to do as he said.

Rescuing the remaining bag and her handbag, she locked the car and brushed past him. But she was intensely conscious of him behind her as she hurried up the path to the house.

If Rachel was conscious of Joe's eyes upon her, Joe was no less aware of it himself. Contrary to the description Charles had invented, Rachel had a decidedly provocative rear. True, she was no fashion model, but that was to her advantage. The cheeks of her bottom were nicely rounded above legs that were longer than he'd thought. For a woman of—what, thirty-two, thirty-three?—she had an extremely attractive figure.

He blew out a breath as he unloaded the bags onto the kitchen table. Why the hell was he thinking about how she looked? It wasn't as if they even knew one another—not, properly at least—and there was no doubt that she resented him. Ever since she'd learned that Daisy would be flying with him and not on some public airline, he'd hardly had a cordial word out of her. Damn it, it wasn't his fault if she and her ex-husband didn't communicate.

'Mr Mendez hasn't been waiting long.' Daisy came into the kitchen behind them, a beaming smile on her face. 'That's good, isn't it, Mum?'

'I'm sure Mr Mendez would agree with you.'

Rachel's response was full of irony, and Joe's resentment stirred anew. 'I did ring first,' he said, directing his words to her. 'I thought you might be working and not want to be disturbed.'

'So you decided to come and disturb me anyway.' Rachel didn't know why she felt so angry, but she did. And finding Mendez on her doorstep seemed to be the last straw after the way Daisy had behaved. 'I'm sorry. I had some shopping to attend to.'

'I could have spoken to Daisy.'

'You could.'

'Mum—'

Daisy had obviously realised that things were not going as

well as she'd anticipated. But Joe didn't need her involvement, any more than Rachel had wanted his earlier. 'Just leave this to your mother and me,' he said, trying for a pleasant tone. 'Why don't you go and do some packing or something?'

Daisy sniffed. 'Mum,' she said again, the word full of entreaty, and Rachel took a deep breath.

'Mr Mendez is right,' she said. 'Perhaps it would be as well if he and I had a private word. Just go up to your room, okay?'

'But, Mum—'

'Do as your mother says,' said Joe sharply, and Daisy's jaw dropped in surprise.

'You can't tell me what to do,' she protested, any admiration she'd felt towards him momentarily extinguished by his tone.

Joe stared at her. 'Can't I?' he countered, his mood deteriorating rapidly, and her lower lip jutted.

'Mum—'

'Oh, just go upstairs, Daisy.' Rachel didn't appreciate Joe's interference either, but it was easier not to get into it with the girl present. 'Please.' She softened the word with a slight smile. 'I'll call you when you can come down again.'

Daisy pursed her lips but, after a few moments, she slouched moodily out of the room. A few seconds later, they heard her climbing the stairs.

Rachel waited until she'd heard the door to Daisy's bedroom bang closed before giving Joe a frigid look. 'I hope you don't expect me to apologise,' she said. 'Thanks to her father, Daisy is in the middle of all this. Naturally, she feels confused.'

'You think?' Joe propped his hips against the counter opposite and folded his arms. 'I thought that was me.'

'You?' Rachel was taken aback now. 'You're not confused.'

Joe shrugged, as if that might be open for discussion, but all he said was, 'I am also in the middle of this feud you've got going with Steve.'

Rachel tried to calm herself. 'It's not a feud.'

'Then what is it?' Joe's dark brows ascended. 'I gather the divorce wasn't an amicable one.'

'Did Steve tell you that?'

He had, but Joe wasn't about to admit it. 'It seems fairly obvious,' he said, avoiding the question. 'Why don't you want Daisy to spend time with her father? Just because you don't get on—'

'I've never stopped Daisy from seeing her father,' Rachel broke in hotly. 'And, if he's told you I have, he's lying.'

Joe sucked in a breath. 'So how come Steve hasn't had any physical contact with Daisy since he left England?'

Rachel gasped. 'I don't have to explain myself to you!'

'Humour me.' Joe didn't really know why he was pursuing this except that she seemed so frustrated. 'You have to admit, it's twelve months since he and Lauren moved to Florida.'

'I know.' Rachel hesitated, but the need to defend herself drove her on. 'But—well, at Christmas, Daisy didn't want to visit her father. Her grandparents would have been so disappointed if we hadn't had Christmas Day with them, and school started again at the beginning of January.'

'Okay.' Joe shrugged. 'I'll accept that you wouldn't want to send Daisy away at Christmas. But according to Steve she could have visited earlier this year.'

'You mean at Easter?' Rachel's nostrils flared. 'Didn't he tell you? Daisy was ill at Easter. She had glandular fever and, if you know anything about the disease at all, you'll know that it can take months to recover fully. As a matter of fact, I phoned Steve and asked if there was any way he could come and see her.' Rachel's nails curled into her palms when she remembered her ex-husband's response. 'He—he said he already had plans for the holiday. Which obviously didn't include crossing the Atlantic.'

Joe frowned 'He didn't tell me that.'

Rachel snorted. 'I wonder why.'

'You don't like him much, do you?'

'I don't like what he's trying to do to me and Daisy,' said Rachel flatly.

'What is he doing?' Joe was curious.

'It doesn't matter.'

'I'd still like to know.'

'Why?' She turned to the bags on the table and started unloading their contents. 'So you can tell Steve what a mean, resentful cow I am when you go home?'

Joe caught his breath. 'Hey, you've got some attitude there!' he exclaimed. 'I don't think you're mean or resentful. I just think you and Steve have got your wires crossed and you both need to sort yourselves out. For Daisy's sake.'

'Yeah, right.'

Rachel had started putting perishable items into the fridge, but now Joe couldn't prevent himself from moving round the table and grabbing her arm. 'Hey,' he said, immediately aware of her soft flesh beneath his fingers. 'I'm not your enemy.' He released her again, unconsciously rubbing his palm down the seam of his jeans, as if that would remove the tantalising memory of her skin. 'I'm just trying to understand what's going on here. Fill me in. Tell me about when Steve still lived in London.'

Rachel shivered. It was the first time he'd touched her, and she was overwhelmingly aware that her response had been far from indifferent. For a moment, her senses had been assaulted by the clean, male scent of his body, his heat briefly robbing her of the will to move away. She was aware of her nipples pebbling beneath her cotton tee shirt, a melting feeling that centred somewhere low in her abdomen, turning her limbs to water.

Realising she had to get a hold of herself, she shoved the pack of cheese she was holding into the fridge and backed up against the closed door. That was better, she thought, feeling the chill cooling her spine and causing goose bumps to take the place of the beads of sweat that had feathered the back of her neck.

Then, without exactly looking at him, she said, 'Why should it matter to you?'

Joe shook his head. Damned if he knew. He didn't know what the hell he was getting into here, but he knew he couldn't just walk away without at least attempting to understand what was going on.

In an effort to distract himself from the urge to capture her chin in his hand and force her to look at him, Joe propped his hips against the table behind him and folded his arms. 'How often did Daisy see her father before he moved to the States?' he asked, and her green eyes flickered briefly in his direction.

'How often?' He sensed she didn't want to answer him and he wondered why. 'Um—she saw him,' she said with a lift of one shoulder, prevaricating. 'Anyway, that's not why you're here, is it? I expect you'd like to confirm the arrangements for Monday. If you'll tell me where and at what time you'd like us to meet you…'

'My chauffeur will pick her up.' Joe was aware that she was nervous, that she'd like to get this over with and for him to go. He frowned, and then asked curiously, 'What's wrong? Why are you so defensive? Is it because Steve wanted to take Daisy to Florida with him when he left England and you wouldn't let him?'

'What?' Rachel was forced to look at him now, stunned at the accusation. And despite her reluctance to discuss her ex-husband with a virtual stranger, she added tensely, 'Steve never even suggested taking her with him. Did he tell you that he did?'

Joe raked long fingers over his scalp. He should never have started this. 'That was the impression I got,' he said at last, watching the colour drain out of her face. His free hand curled into a fist. 'Obviously I was wrong.'

'Yes.' Rachel drew a choking breath and turned away, unable to look at him any longer. 'Yes, you were,' she continued, pressing her palms against the door of the fridge now, aware that it wasn't helping. 'If—if you must know, I don't think Daisy even noticed when Steve left the country.'

There, she'd said it. Something she'd never said to anyone, not even Steve's mother. But it was true nevertheless. Her ex-husband had spent little time with Daisy when they'd been together, and after the divorce he'd always been too busy with his new wife and her friends—and, of course, his golf—to care that Daisy was growing up without a father.

Joe stifled an inward groan. He knew he'd upset her, knew he'd torn the skin off an old wound that was apparently still raw enough to bleed. And that wasn't his nature. He didn't hurt women; even the women he'd ended relationships with were still speaking to him. Yet, although he'd guessed he was getting into deep water when she'd avoided his question, he'd persisted in probing, in exposing her vulnerability.

His muscles tightened. He should get the hell out of here now, before he did something they would both regret. He didn't even know why he felt such a sense of responsibility towards her, but the fact remained, he did.

Pushing away from the table, he laid an impulsive hand on her shoulder. She jumped, and he realised she was trembling. God, this was a woman who'd been married and divorced, who'd borne a child, for heaven's sake; yet he still felt responsible for her. He couldn't resist; his fingers tightened on the fine bones beneath her tee shirt and the urge to pull her into his arms became almost irresistible.

The air between them was fairly crackling with emotion, and for once he wished Daisy would interrupt them. Hell, this wasn't his problem, he told himself, but that didn't stop him from moving closer until her bottom brushed temptingly against his thigh.

Rachel moved then, jerking away from him, not under-standing why her eyes were suddenly filled with tears. She'd shed all the tears she was going to shed for Steve Carlyle, she told herself fiercely. And she didn't need Joe Mendez's pity either. She could just imagine how this would play when he got back to Florida, and the idea that Steve and Lauren might find her stupid feelings amusing was totally humiliating.

'Rachel,' Joe said helplessly, 'I'm sorry.'

'Don't be. I'm not.' She pulled a tissue out of the box on the window sill and quickly blew her nose. 'I'll get Daisy. I expect she's dying to know what's going on.'

Joe groaned. 'What is going on, Rachel?' he demanded, and she was obliged to turn and face him.

'I don't know what you mean,' she said, striving for a lighter tone. But when she attempted to move past him, Joe saw the betraying sparkle of tears on her lashes.

'Hell, Rachel,' he protested, and ignoring all the good advice he'd been giving himself, he caught her about the waist and hauled her into his arms.

CHAPTER FIVE

It was meant to be a way of comforting her, of showing his support, of proving he wasn't a selfish bastard like her ex-husband appeared to be, or so he told himself. But it didn't turn out that way. From the moment their bodies came together, from the moment her tee shirt parted from her jeans and he felt the softness of bare flesh beneath his hands, a knot of pure sensual need twisted in his belly.

She was breathing rapidly, her breasts flattened against his chest so he could feel every agitated gulp she took. Her lips were parted and the warmth of her breath was moistening the skin of his throat, spreading heat to every sensitised extremity.

'Rachel,' he said again, his voice thicker now, and the urge to slide his hand beneath her shirt and find the swollen peaks that were rubbing oh-so-sensuously against his shirt proved irresistible. He could see the pulse palpitating just beneath her ear, and he wondered how it would feel against his tongue.

He thought she said something then, but the faint whisper of her voice was drowned by the pounding of his own heart. With the womanly scent of her body to distract him, it was hard to think of anything but how incredible it would feel to have her naked beneath him.

He was becoming aroused. His trousers were becoming uncomfortably tight, and he guessed if he could feel it she could feel it, too. Not that that stopped him from wanting her, but it was time to grasp what little control he had left and put an end to this madness.

It took an effort, but he pulled his hands from beneath her tee shirt and raised them to her shoulders. Then gently, but firmly, he attempted to put some space between them. It would be easier to think without the innocent sexuality of her body seducing his, he told himself grimly. But when he saw her face, his good intentions crumbled. She looked so bewildered suddenly that something inside him seemed to snap. With a groan of resignation, he abandoned any hope of getting out of this unscathed. Pulling her against him again, he captured her face between his palms and lowered his head to hers.

Her lips were barely parted, but when he skimmed his tongue over the full lower one she caught her breath. Joe pushed his tongue inside, searching, possessing, doing what he admitted he'd wanted to do since he'd first glimpsed those tears on her face.

'Dear God,' he muttered, as desire rose hotly to the surface. His hands slid down her spine, moulding her to him, finding the provocative curve of her bottom before gripping the back of her thighs.

The kiss deepened and Rachel's world seemed to narrow to this man's mouth, this man's hands. Her head was swimming, emotions she'd never experienced before causing her whole body to feel hot and alive. She was drowning in a dark sea of intimacy, of passion, where the satisfaction of her senses was the only thing that mattered.

Joe's senses rocketed, the blood pounding in his ears, his mind spinning dizzily out of control. With his fingers spreading against the back of her head, he crushed his mouth to hers with increasing urgency. He wasn't doing anything wrong, he told himself. Not when she was kissing him back with a hunger that matched his own.

And then, from a distance, Rachel heard a familiar voice calling her. 'Mum! Mum!' There was a pause, which allowed her to identify the sound. 'Mum, can't I come down now?'

Daisy!

Oh God!

Rachel's strangled cry startled Joe. He, too, had heard the other voice, his brain scrambling to remember where he was. Then, like a douche of cold water, it came to him: he was trying to seduce Steve Carlyle's ex-wife.

He pulled away automatically at the same moment Rachel was wrenching herself free. For God's sake, what had he been thinking? What crazy impulse had made him behave like a savage?

Rachel was heading for the door into the hall. He could see she was panicking, unaware that her tee shirt was loose and crumpled and that his stubble had scraped her cheeks. Her hair was loose from its knot. It tumbled down around her shoulders, and Joe wondered how it would feel if he threaded his fingers through the silky strands. However, the look she cast at him over her shoulder brought the whole situation into damning focus.

He'd goofed, and badly. Her expression said it all. And while he wasn't totally to blame for what had happened, if he hadn't touched her the situation would never have developed as it had.

'Hey,' he said, causing her to glance back at him again. However, when she lifted a warning hand to silence him, he muttered, 'You might want to check yourself out before you leave. Or do you want your daughter to know what you've been doing?'

Rachel halted abruptly, her hand going to her tumbled hair, discovering the pins that had held it in place had disappeared. They were scattered all over the floor, she saw with an inward groan, but she didn't have time to find them all now. Pulling open a drawer where she kept pens and notepads, she found an elastic band and, gathering her hair in one hand, she secured it in an untidy pony-tail.

She saw Joe arch a mocking brow as she started for the door again, but her attention was concentrated on her daughter now. 'Just—just give us a couple more minutes, Daisy,' she called when she reached the doorway. 'We're almost through.'

Ain't that the truth? thought Joe as Daisy answered with a long drawn-out, 'O-kay.' Once again, he was asking himself how on earth he'd allowed himself to be distracted. Rachel was attractive, sure, but she wasn't his type. And from the way she was looking at him, he certainly wasn't hers.

She turned back to him with evident reluctance. He sensed she wanted to say something to defend herself, but she must know as well as he did that what had happened couldn't be explained away. 'I think you'd better go,' she said at last, and he could tell she was struggling to appear more composed than she was. She licked her lips, lips that were still swollen from his lovemaking, Joe saw with some satisfaction. 'I don't know what I'm going to do about Daisy. I'll let you know when I've had time to think.'

'To think about what?' Joe sagged back against the table. 'Oh, please, don't tell me you're going to make this an excuse for refusing to let Daisy go and visit with her dad?'

'No.' Rachel squared her shoulders. 'No, she can go. I'm just not sure she should go with you.'

Joe stared at her disbelievingly. 'Why?' he demanded, his patience shredding. Frustration was making him antsy, and he wasn't in the mood for any more of her attitude. 'I hope you're not implying that because I kissed you I'm not to be trusted with your daughter. Grow up, Rachel. You're acting like a spoiled brat.'

'And we both know that's not true, don't we?' she retorted. She shook her head. 'I have to think about this. I'm older than you. I can't just dismiss what just happened as you apparently can.'

Joe blinked. 'Why do you think you're older than me?' he exclaimed blankly. 'I'm thirty-four, and I know for a fact that Steve's only thirty-five.'

'Steve's not thirty-five!' The words were out before she could prevent them. 'He's two years older than me. He'll be forty on his next birthday.'

Joe looked surprised. 'You're sure about that?' he asked, and she wondered if she'd put her foot in it again.

'I'm sure,' she admitted in a low voice, and Joe realised he hadn't taken Daisy's age into consideration. He remembered Steve telling him in one of his more confidential moments that he'd been married for five years before Daisy had been born.

Rachel had opened the fridge again and was stowing some tomatoes into the salad drawer. Her face was red, and he wondered what she was thinking. For his part, he was trying to come to terms with the fact that she was thirty-seven. She certainly didn't look it. Or act it, he conceded, reliving those moments when he'd been inclined to believe she was as inexperienced as Daisy.

'Look,' he said gently. 'I'm sorry, okay? What happened, happened. I'm not ashamed of it. You're a beautiful woman. I only did what any man in my position would have done.'

Rachel wondered if that was entirely true. She couldn't imagine Steve touching her in that way. But then, she and Steve should never have got married, never have had a baby. It was one of those sad anomalies that Daisy definitely hadn't kept them together.

'Is everything all right?' Daisy was suddenly standing in the doorway, eyeing them both with a mixture of anticipation and apprehension. She frowned at her mother. 'Why is your face red? Is something wrong?'

Rachel couldn't prevent her hand from going to her cheek,

and she glanced guiltily at Joe before saying, 'Nothing's wrong, Daisy. Mr Mendez was just leaving.'

Daisy wasn't stupid. 'Leaving?' she echoed. 'So—are the arrangements for Monday already made?'

'You'd better ask your mother,' said Joe, without sympathy. 'I think she might be having second thoughts.'

He knew a moment's remorse when Rachel turned agonised eyes in his direction, but he refused to pretend that all was well when it so obviously wasn't.

'Why?' Daisy gazed at her mother now. 'I thought you'd agreed to let me go.'

'I did.' Rachel was defensive. 'It's just—'

'Your mother doesn't trust me,' said Joe flatly, pushing away from the table. His eyes bruised Rachel's. 'I suggest you let me know when you've decided what you want to do.'

'Oh, but—'

Daisy's eyes had filled with tears and, before she could beg him to reconsider, Rachel intervened. 'There's no need for that,' she said stiffly. 'Just tell me where and at what time you'd like us to meet you on Monday and we'll be there.'

Joe blew out a breath. 'My chauffeur will pick her up about nine o'clock Monday morning,' he responded. 'If you change your mind again, let me know.'

Shelley was waiting at Eaton Court Mews when he got back.

She'd evidently been there for some time, because a tray of coffee was cold on the table and her face mirrored her impatience with his behaviour earlier.

'Where the hell have you been?' she demanded as soon as he strolled into the sitting room. 'What do you mean by walking out like that? I go to sleep with you beside me and I wake up to find you've gone.'

'Sorry.' But Joe wasn't in the mood to make more apologies and when Charles followed him into the room he turned with some relief. 'Black coffee, please,' he said. 'And perhaps Ms Adair might like to join me. Oh, and do you have any of those English muffins? I could do with something hot and sweet.'

'I hope you're not looking at me,' said Shelley, her tone softening as if she realised this was not the time to start a slanging match. But Joe only shook his head and lounged into a comfortable leather armchair.

'Just food,' he said, and Charles withdrew before another argument ensued.

However, realising he was allowing his frustration towards Rachel to influence his mood, Joe looked up at Shelley standing by the window. 'Have you been here long?'

She shrugged. Although he'd only thrown his clothes on before leaving her apartment, she had evidently taken some trouble with her appearance. A pale blue gauze dress dipped provocatively at her breast before flaring gently to her knees. Four-inch heels added height to her five-feet-ten-inch frame, and her blonde bob had been spiked to perfection. Evidently she'd dressed to please, and he felt guilty that right at this moment her pale good looks left him cold.

'Long enough,' she said now, moving over to his chair and perching on the arm. 'You need a shave, darling. I'm not one of those women who like getting the equivalent of razor burns every time I kiss you.'

Unwanted, the image of Rachel as he'd last seen her flashed into his mind. How was it possible that he'd found her so appealing? So appealing, in fact, that if her daughter hadn't interrupted them...

'Joe, you're not listening to me!' Shelley's voice rose again, and now there were hectic splashes of colour in her cheeks. 'Where have you been? Charles is so tight-lipped. He wouldn't breathe a word.'

'That's what I pay him for,' said Joe laconically, making no response when she slipped her arm around his neck. 'There was something I had to do. An arrangement I had to make for Monday. One of the guys back home asked me to fly his daughter over and I needed to check it out.'

Shelley's shoulders stiffened. 'His daughter?'

'Yeah, his daughter.' Joe glanced up at her. 'You got an objection?'

'Several.' Shelley's eyes flashed. 'To start with, how old is she?'

'Gee, let me see.' Joe pretended to think about it, hoping the distraction would lighten his mood as well as hers. 'In her teens, I guess.'

'Her teens?' Shelley's voice rose even higher.

'Yeah. Thirteen, I think. I can't remember.'

'Oh!' Her relief was evident, but when she bent to rub her lips against his Joe didn't take the bait.

'It's gonna be a busy weekend,' he said, forcing her to draw back just as Charles came back into the room. 'Ah, food! You ought to try one of these muffins, Shell. Charles makes them himself, and they're magic.'

'I'm glad you find something magical,' retorted Shelley huffily, getting to her feet again and surveying him with angry blue eyes. 'I hope this doesn't mean I won't see you again before you leave.'

'Shell—'

'I've brought two cups in case Ms Adair decides to join you,' Charles interposed swiftly as he set down the tray. He walked back to the door. 'Let me know if you need anything else.'

'Thanks.' As Charles disappeared again, Joe shifted forward and broke a piece off one of the warm muffins. In actual fact, he wasn't particularly hungry, but it was a way to avoid Shelley's accusing gaze. 'Come on,' he invited. 'Try a piece.'

'You know I don't eat fatty things,' replied Shelley stiffly. 'And you shouldn't either. They're bad for your cholesterol.'

Joe pulled a wry face. 'Oh, I think it can stand one English muffin,' he murmured drily. 'I promise to use the gym as soon as I get home.'

Shelley's lips pursed. 'You love making fun of me, don't you?'

'No.' Joe reached for the pot of coffee. 'But you sound as if you've had a sense of humour bypass.'

Shelley sucked in a breath. 'I don't understand you, Joe. When you first got here, you couldn't wait to see me. Then, last night, you lost consciousness as soon as your head hit the pillow.'

'I was tired.' There was a distinct edge to Joe's voice now, but Shelley didn't seem to notice.

'You can't have been that tired,' she retorted. 'You were up early enough this morning. You left the apartment without even waking me. I don't think you even took a shower. You certainly didn't leave a message. What was I supposed to think?'

Joe's jaw clamped. She was right, but he didn't like hearing about it. He didn't like the idea that anything that had happened since his arrival in England a week ago should have had any effect on his behaviour. He couldn't tell her he'd left her bed because he'd been having a hot, sweaty dream about another woman. And this morning he'd suffered a serious lapse of judgment, that was all. It certainly wasn't terminal.

'I've said I'm sorry,' he muttered tersely, reaching for his coffee and swallowing it black. He needed a jolt of caffeine to kick-start his brain. He also needed to get his head around the fact that a feisty female with tear-filled green eyes hadn't permanently rocked his reason.

'So…' Shelley's tongue circled her glossy lips. 'Will I see you tonight?'

Joe blew out a breath. 'Not tonight, no.'

'Why not?'

'Because I've promised this guy whose daughter I was telling you about that I'd go and check on his family.'

'His family?'

'His ma and pa.'

Shelley snorted. 'I don't believe you.'

'Your call. But it's true.' He paused. 'You can come with me, if you like.' That way if, by some unlucky chance Rachel should be there...

But he hadn't finished the thought before Shelley broke in. 'You've got to be joking! You want me to spend Saturday night visiting some old couple who're probably senile?' She snorted. 'Give me a break.'

'Okay.' Joe didn't argue. 'Then I guess I'll see you Sunday night before I leave.'

Shelley groaned. 'You know I've got to attend that awards dinner on Sunday evening. I told you at the start of the week.'

'Then I guess we won't see one another until you come to the Caribbean for your photo shoot in November.'

Shelley sulked. 'Couldn't you get out of this visit? For me? Please!'

'Couldn't you miss the awards dinner?' he countered.

'You know I can't.'

Joe shrugged, ashamed to find he was half relieved. 'Impasse,' he said. 'Come on. Drink your coffee. I'm sure you'll have no difficulty finding another man to spend your evening with.'

Shelley stalked across the floor. 'You're a bastard, do you know that?'

'So I've been told,' murmured Joe mildly, but the only response he got was the slamming of the door.

CHAPTER SIX

RACHEL was typing a page of her novel for the umpteenth time when the phone rang.

'Oh, great,' she muttered broodingly, aware that the story wasn't going as it should, and that her agent was probably ringing to check on its possible completion.

'Yes?' she said, the frustration evident in her voice.

And then she pulled a wry face when Evelyn Carlyle said tartly, 'I'm sorry if I'm being a nuisance.'

'Oh, of course you're not.' Rachel was contrite. Since Daisy had left for Florida over a week ago, her in-laws had been a constant source of support. 'I thought it was Marcia. She's been grumbling because I haven't got the manuscript finished.'

'Oh, I see.' Evelyn sounded mollified. 'I should have guessed. You looked tired yesterday. Aren't you sleeping well?'

'Well enough,' said Rachel tersely, aware that it was the man who'd escorted her daughter to Florida, not her manuscript, that was disrupting her sleep. It didn't help to know that, when he'd called on Howard and Evelyn as he'd promised Steve, they'd found him a very personable young man. Evelyn had even expressed the opinion that it was a pity Daisy wasn't older, which had really set Rachel's nerves on edge. 'I just wish Daisy would keep in touch,' she added now, but her mother-in-law was dismissive.

'You know what girls are like. She'll be enjoying herself and calling home will come very low on her list. Besides, Steve would have been on the phone if there was anything wrong.'

Was that supposed to reassure her? For once, Rachel wasn't in the mood to see Daisy's point of view. 'All the same,' she said tensely, 'I think she could have made an effort to send me a postcard, at least. She sent me an email when she arrived, but that's all.'

'And you're missing her. I know.' Evelyn was more sympathetic. 'And Howard and I are no substitute for your little girl. But she's growing up, Rachel. She'll be off to college before you know it. Visiting her father is probably a good thing. It will get you used to her being away.'

'She's only thirteen, Lynnie.'

Rachel couldn't help defending herself, and the older woman sighed. 'Yes. Yes, I know. But the years go by so quickly.' She paused. 'Anyway, didn't you tell me you'd had a call from Paul Davis?'

Rachel sighed. Paul Davis was the man she used to work for before her writing career had taken off. After the divorce she'd had to get a full-time job to help support herself and Daisy, and Paul had been a good employer. The trouble was, he wanted to be more than that, and he'd taken to calling every few weeks to ask her how she was and, occasionally, ask her out.

And she had been tempted to accept his invitation recently, mostly to get Evelyn off her back. Not that her mother-in-law wanted her to get married again. She still nurtured hopes that she and Steve would get back together.

'Yes, he rang,' she said now, resignation setting in at the thought of what was coming next.

'So why don't you go out with him?' Evelyn asked encouragingly. 'He's a nice young man, isn't he? And you deserve some entertainment while Daisy's away.'

'He's hardly *young*,' said Rachel drily. 'He's fifty or there-abouts. And he's never been married, Lynnie. He still lives with his widowed mother.'

'Which shows how dependable he is,' declared Evelyn firmly. 'Come on, Rachel. When did you last have a date?'

Too long ago to remember, thought Rachel ruefully as the memory of that scene with Joe Mendez flashed back into her mind. Sometimes she wondered if that had all been a figment of her imagination too. There was no doubt that it had been an unlikely event.

But then she remembered the nights during the past week when she'd awakened to find her breasts taut and sensitive, and an ache twisting low in her stomach that wouldn't go away. Sometimes she was soaked with sweat, too, her night-shirt clinging wetly to her aroused body. That wasn't her imagination, she knew, and she'd found it very hard to get back to sleep.

'Rachel!'

She'd been silent too long and Evelyn was getting impa-tient. 'I'm here,' she said. 'I was just thinking, perhaps I should go out with Paul.' *Liar!* 'It may be just what I need.' *To get Joe Mendez out of her head.*

'Oh, good.' Evelyn was pleased, evidently thinking her per-suasion had worked. 'Let me know what happens, won't you, dear? Howard and I only have your best interests in mind.'

Rachel hung up the phone, wondering if agreeing to go out with Paul had been rather foolish. But she could hardly admit that the last time she'd slept with a man had been after the divorce papers had been delivered. Accepting an invitation to one of Julie Corbett's parties as a way of getting out of the house had been stupid. Finding herself in Julie's bedroom after one too many vodka martinis with a man she'd thank-fully not seen either before or since had been downright stupid.

Fortunately she hadn't been too drunk to ensure he'd used

protection, but for weeks afterwards she'd worried in case it hadn't been enough. Still, nothing untoward had happened, but it had been a sobering experience. One she'd vowed would never happen again.

Rachel bought a new outfit for her dinner date with Paul Davis. The low-cut crocheted top and skirt were a delicate shade of turquoise, and complemented the sun-streaked colour of her hair. The top also revealed a tantalising glimpse of cleavage, while the short skirt didn't exaggerate the provocative curve of her hips. The slightly cropped top also skimmed her midriff, as she appreciated every time she moved and a draught of cooler air brushed against her skin.

But the date itself was a disaster. As Rachel realised halfway through the evening when Paul had talked of nothing but his vintage Jaguar, and the extensive model-railway he had laid out in his mother's attic. She wished she'd asked Evelyn to ring her, to give her an escape if any was necessary. As it was, she could see the remainder of the evening stretching ahead of her without any relief from Paul's hobbies.

She had just begun to say she didn't want a dessert, in the hope of cutting the evening short, when her mobile phone started ringing. Knowing Evelyn's penchant for gossip, she guessed her mother-in-law was impatient to hear how she was enjoying herself. Or perhaps she'd heard from Daisy, she thought, glad of any distraction. But when she heard Evelyn's voice, she knew immediately that something was wrong.

'Hello, Lynnie,' she said, hoping she was mistaken. 'This is a surprise.'

'Oh, darling.' Evelyn sounded unlike herself. 'I'm sorry to interrupt your evening. Are you having a good time?'

Not really, thought Rachel. But she said, 'It's fine.' She cast an unwilling glance in Paul's direction. 'What is it, Lynnie? Is something wrong?'

But she knew. Before Evelyn spoke, she felt an uneasy shiver slide down her spine. 'I just thought you'd want to know, that's all,' said her mother-in-law as Rachel's brain raced ahead to a dozen probable scenarios, all of them bad. 'We've had a call from Steve.'

'Steve?' The fingers of apprehension tightened their hold around Rachel's stomach. This must be something to do with Daisy, she thought. Was this why she hadn't heard from her daughter recently? Oh God, she begged, please don't let anything bad have happened to her.

'Rachel!' Paul was speaking to her now, and she looked at him with uncomprehending eyes. 'The waiter wants to know what you'd like for dessert,' he said impatiently. 'He hasn't got all night.'

Rachel blinked. 'Not now,' she told him unsteadily. Then, to Evelyn, 'What is it? What's happened? Is Daisy hurt?'

'Not seriously, I'm sure.' Evelyn sounded as if she half wished she hadn't made the call now. 'There's been an accident…'

'Rachel!'

It was Paul speaking to her again, but Rachel ignored him. 'What kind of accident?' she demanded raggedly. 'When did it happen?'

'Oh, I'm not sure. Yesterday, the day before—Steve didn't say.' Evelyn tried to calm her. 'They were all out on Lauren's father's yacht, apparently. I don't think it's anything to worry about, but—'

Rachel sucked in a breath. She'd known. She'd positively known that Daisy would have been in touch if she could. 'I'm coming home,' she said. 'Right now. I want to speak to Steve myself. I want to know exactly how it happened and why I wasn't told at once.'

'Um…' There was something more, but Evelyn evidently thought better of telling her then. 'Yes, perhaps you should come home,' she agreed. 'Then we can discuss all the details.'

Rachel wanted to say 'What details?' but it would be easier to wait until she could speak to her mother-in-law face to face. 'I'll be about twenty minutes.'

She closed her phone to find Paul staring at her disbelievingly. 'What's going on?' he asked as she pushed back her chair. 'You're not leaving?'

'I'm afraid I am.' Rachel took a breath. 'That was Steve's mother. Daisy's had an accident. I've got to go home so I can call her.'

Paul didn't look pleased. 'I'll drive you,' he said, but she could tell it was the last thing he wanted to do. He'd been enjoying his meal and, judging by his slight paunch, food played a large part in his enjoyment of life. Along with his car and model railway, of course.

'There's no need,' she said now, gathering up her wrap from the back of her chair. 'You finish your meal. I can get a taxi. Thanks for—for everything. I'll probably see you later.'

CHAPTER SEVEN

THE British Airways flight to Miami had been due to land at three o'clock local time, but the airport was busy, and they'd had to circle the immediate area at least twice before being given permission to make an approach. Then, after landing, there were all the usual formalities to attend to, more thorough than ever now since the increase in terrorism, so that it was almost five o'clock when Rachel emerged into the arrivals hall.

She was tired. She'd hardly slept the night before and, although lots of her fellow passengers had slept during the long flight, she'd remained upright in her seat, replaying all she'd learned since Evelyn had rung her at the restaurant.

She'd arrived at the in-laws' house prepared for the worst, and she hadn't been disappointed. What Evelyn hadn't told her on the phone was that Daisy was in a hospital in Palm Cove, which was about twelve miles from downtown Miami. She'd apparently fallen from the Johansens' yacht and hit her head on the bathing platform as she'd gone into the water. Fortunately, one of the crew had realised something was wrong when she hadn't surfaced and he'd dived in after her. He'd managed to bring Daisy back to the surface, but she'd swallowed a lot of water. She'd been unconscious when they'd pulled her back on board.

Rachel had been horrified. Her first thought had been, why

hadn't Steve noticed what had happened? But that hadn't been a question Evelyn could answer. And Steve, when she'd finally tracked him down at the Johansens' house, had been similarly obtuse. 'She's thirteen, for God's sake,' he'd snapped angrily. 'She doesn't need a nursemaid twenty-four-seven.'

Rachel had made no comment about this. She could have said that Daisy should have been wearing a life jacket, which she obviously hadn't been; that, as she'd never been out on a yacht before, he might have taken the trouble to keep an eye on her. But she'd never had much success in arguments with Steve, and she hadn't intended to try now. Instead she'd said, 'I'd like to see her. Would you have any objections if I flew out and visited her myself?'

Steve had been surprisingly agreeable. 'Why not?' he'd said carelessly. 'That's why I rang the old lady. I knew you'd start clucking like a mother hen. If you want to come, I won't stop you.'

As if he could, Rachel had thought grimly, but at least he couldn't accuse her of acting without his knowledge. And when she'd come off the phone, Evelyn had confided that Steve had admitted that Daisy had been asking for her. That was why she'd taken the liberty of interrupting her date.

Now, dragging her suitcase behind her, Rachel made for the exit. The concourse was crowded and she was anticipating a lengthy wait for a taxi when someone caught her arm.

'Rachel,' a familiar voice said. 'I thought I must have missed you.'

It was Joe Mendez, and Rachel stared at him with disbelieving eyes. 'Joe!' she exclaimed without thinking. And then, 'I mean—Mr Mendez. What are you doing here?'

'Didn't I make myself clear?' Joe gave her a rueful smile. 'I came to meet you.' He glanced down at her suitcase. 'Is this all your luggage?'

'I—yes, but—'

'Good. Let's go.' He took the handle from her unresisting fingers. 'We can talk in the car. It's just outside.'

Rachel blinked. 'Um—did Steve ask you to meet me?'

'It was my decision,' said Joe, steering her round a portly woman whose tight jeans emphasised her size. 'Did you have a good journey?'

Rachel made some reply, but her mind wasn't really on her words. He was the last person she'd expected to see at the airport—or anywhere else, for that matter. She'd found a modest hotel in Palm Cove and booked herself a room via the Internet. The hotel wasn't far from the hospital, and it would be easy for her to visit Daisy without making any demands on anyone.

She certainly didn't expect to spend any time with her ex-husband. She'd accepted that they might run into one another at the hospital, but that was all. She was here for one reason and one reason only, and that was to see her daughter. At present, that was the only thing on her mind.

The humidity hit her as soon as they stepped out of the terminal. Until then, the air-conditioning had cushioned her from the oppressive heat outside. Heavy clouds hung over the airport buildings, dark and threatening, and a damp warmth moistened the skin at the back of her neck and sapped what little strength she had left.

A sleek black limousine idled in a no-waiting zone, and Joe headed straight for it, evidently expecting her to follow him. A uniformed chauffeur sprang out at their approach and swung open the rear doors of the car. Then, taking the suitcase Joe had been carrying, he flipped the boot lid and dropped the case inside.

Joe turned and for the first time she was able to take a proper look at him. In a tight-fitting black tee shirt and khaki cargo-shorts, he looked nothing like the CEO of a successful computer company that she knew him to be. Amazingly, his hair had grown a little in the week or so since she'd seen him, but there was the same shadow of stubble on his jawline.

'D'you want to get in?' he suggested, taking charge of the door nearest to him, and Rachel decided not to argue at this time. Although he probably had dispensation to park his vehicle in the area primarily given over to hire cars and taxis, she didn't want to be responsible for him earning a fine.

It was deliciously cool in the limousine, the soft leather giving luxuriously beneath her weight. There was enough room in front of her to stretch out full-length if she wanted to, and for the first time since leaving home she felt herself relax.

It didn't last long. When Joe circled the car and swung in beside her, she stiffened automatically. She could smell his heat, and his maleness, and the front of his shirt was just the slightest bit damp, as if he'd been sweating.

His knee brushed her thigh as he lounged on the seat beside her, bare legs brown and muscular and liberally spread with dark hair. The hairs on his arms were dark too, and once again she could see the shadow of the tattoo that was almost hidden by the short sleeve of his shirt. He looked lean and powerful, and totally at ease.

And just like that her pulse quickened, and she felt a melting heat between her legs. Despite her worries about Daisy, her body had a will of its own. Her breathing grew shallow and she prayed he wouldn't notice. Or if he did that he'd put it down to the suffocating heat outside.

'Okay,' he said as the chauffeur got behind the wheel and they started away from the kerb. 'Did Steve fix you up with a hotel?'

Rachel moistened her lips and smoothed her damp palms over the knees of her cotton trousers. 'I fixed myself up, actually,' she said. 'It's just a small hotel. The *Park Plaza*; I believe it's near the hospital.'

'The *Park Plaza?*' Joe's brows drew together. 'I don't believe I know it.' He leaned forward and addressed the chauffeur. 'Have you heard of the *Park Plaza* hotel in Palm Cove, Luther?' he asked, and the other man nodded.

'Yes, sir,' he said. 'It's on Spanish Avenue. Near the shopping mall.'

'Oh, yeah.' Joe seemed to recognise the location even if the hotel was unfamiliar to him. 'Okay, head in that direction.'

'Yes, sir.'

Luther acknowledged his instructions, and then Joe pressed a button in the arm of the door beside him and the privacy screen slid up between them and the chauffeur. 'Now,' he said, 'I guess you'd like to know how Daisy is this afternoon?' He paused, and when she widened her eyes he added, 'I saw her myself earlier today, and she seems to be making steady progress.'

'Thank God!'

Rachel's response was heartfelt and Joe regarded her with sympathetic eyes. It couldn't have been easy, he thought, learning that her daughter—who'd happened to be four thousand miles away at the time—had suffered a blow to the head that had needed specialist treatment. Joe himself, who'd been prepared, had been shocked when he'd seen the kid. Her face was covered in bruises and one of her eyes was almost completely closed.

'So.' Rachel knew she had to say something. 'How did you come to meet me? I could have taken a cab, you know.'

'Yeah.' Joe shrugged. 'And you could have been waiting a couple hours. I thought you might be glad to see a friendly face.'

'Are you a friendly face?' Rachel looked doubtful.

'I thought so.'

Rachel caught the inner side of her lower lip between her teeth. 'I suppose you're hoping I'll apologise. For—for what happened.'

'Oh, yeah.' Joe's eyes widened. 'And I'm expecting hell to freeze over any minute.' He shook his head. 'I could tell you

I'm sorry, but that wouldn't be true. I wanted to kiss you and I did.' For a moment, his fingers skimmed sensually against her cheek. 'I guess what you really want me to say is that it won't happen again.'

Did she?

Rachel drew back automatically, but he'd already withdrawn his hand. Lounging on the seat beside her, he was like a predator at bay. Yet he didn't scare her. She scared herself. Her skin was still prickling with the memory of his touch.

Knowing she had to say something, she chose a casual tone. 'That would be good,' she said. 'I wouldn't like you to think I'd taken it too seriously.' Although she had! 'I've not exactly been celibate since my divorce.'

Joe regarded her through his lashes. Now why didn't he believe her? he wondered. Her mouth had been hot, hotter than he'd ever imagined it would be, and her response had been all he'd wanted and more. God, if Daisy hadn't been lurking upstairs, he didn't know how far he might have taken it. He'd certainly been aching with the need to bury himself between her legs.

Yet, for all that, there'd been an innocence about the way she'd reacted that didn't gel with the image she was trying to convey now. He had the feeling it was a long time since she'd felt the need to portray herself as an experienced woman. She was trying to be brash, trying to show he hadn't scraped a nerve, but her eyes told an entirely different story. And he felt an almost overwhelming need to show her how wrong she was.

Big mistake.

'Okay,' he said, deciding to let it go for now, even if he was aware that he had a hard-on there was no way he was going to relieve. Thank heavens for baggy shorts, he thought wryly, adjusting his underwear. 'So I guess you'd rather I hadn't come to meet you, yeah?'

'Oh...no.' Rachel knew if she was going to carry this off

she had to act naturally. 'It was—it was very kind of you to put yourself out.'

'I don't look at it as putting myself out,' said Joe firmly, though he had to ask himself why he'd been so eager to come. Steve had put him in the picture and he had been concerned for Daisy, naturally, but wanting to see Rachel again was something else. And he knew it.

Rachel turned her head and tried to concentrate on the view beyond the limousine's windows. They were travelling along a wide road with tall trees growing on either side. On her right, beyond the belt of palms, the Atlantic reflected the overcast sky. Yet could it really be the Atlantic? It looked too placid to be the ocean.

The silence between them was pregnant with tension, and, forcing herself to relax, she said, 'Do you live in Miami, Mr Mendez?'

'It's Joe,' he amended mildly. Then, 'It's not my permanent address, no. But I have a condo out on Miami Beach that I use when I'm visiting the city.'

Rachel wanted to ask where his permanent address was, but it wasn't anything to do with her. Nevertheless, remembering how impressed Daisy had been by the house she'd visited in London, she couldn't prevent herself from saying, with unknowing wistfulness, 'I expect you have a lot of homes.'

'One or two,' he conceded, not wanting to talk about himself. 'Tell me, when did you hear about the accident?'

Rachel's eyes widened. 'Last night. Why?'

Joe managed to hide his astonishment. The kid's accident had occurred three days ago. In Steve's place, he'd have let Rachel know at once. Particularly in the circumstances. 'I guess you must have booked your seat on the next flight?'

'Yes, I did.'

Rachel felt troubled now. Joe's expression wasn't always

readable, but there was something in his face that made her add urgently, 'Why do you ask?'

'No reason.'

Joe's eyes darkened, lingering on her face with a warmth and intensity that brought an embarrassing wave of colour into her cheeks. Looking at him now, she could hardly believe how intimate they'd once been. And while he was probably used to doing whatever the hell he liked, she most definitely wasn't.

Only he mustn't know that.

Dragging her eyes away from his lean, disturbing face, she forced herself to remember why she was here: Daisy. Her daughter should be her prime concern, and she doubted she'd be too impressed to learn that her mother was dwelling on the possible actions of a man she'd convinced herself she didn't even like. Although with his hip only inches from hers, and the remembered awareness of how he'd made her feel when he'd thrust his tongue into her mouth, those sentiments seemed decidedly suspect.

She felt so hot suddenly, a bead of sweat trickling down between her breasts. Which was ridiculous, considering the coolness of the car. To distract herself, she tried to find some interest in the buildings that lined the other side of the wide boulevard: neo-classical styles fighting for space between modern high-rises, the occasional square of parkland a welcome splash of greenery.

'Um, Palm Cove,' she murmured, aware that Joe was still watching her. 'Is it much farther?'

'Not far.' Joe shifted forward in his seat and her heart leapt into her throat. But although his thigh briefly brushed hers, all he did was open a small chilled cabinet set beneath the polished console opposite. Inside was a selection of sodas and mixers, and gesturing, he said, 'Are you thirsty?'

Rachel's mouth was dry, but she doubted a drink would

cure it. Still, the sight of the frosted bottles was appealing, and she said a little breathlessly, 'Do you have mineral water?'

'Water?' Joe studied the contents of the cabinet. 'Yeah, sure. There you go.' He handed her a bottle. 'You need a glass?'

'Oh—no.' Rachel unscrewed the cap with some difficulty. Her fingers were hot and slippery, but thankfully he didn't offer to do it for her. 'This is fine.'

'Good.' Joe closed the cabinet again and lounged back in his seat. Then, his eyes on the slender column of her throat visible above the open neck of her cotton shirt, he added, 'You do know that's where Steve and Lauren live? Palm Cove, I mean.'

Rachel almost choked on the water. 'No,' she gasped, when she was able. 'No, I didn't.' The last address she'd been given was the apartment—or condo—they'd occupied in Miami itself.

'Oh, yeah.' Joe wondered what else Steve hadn't told her. 'They share the Johansen mansion with Lauren's old man. His wife died a couple of years ago, and I guess he got tired of rattling round that old place on his own.'

Rachel's tongue circled her lips. 'So Daisy's been staying there, too?'

Joe frowned. 'That bothers you?'

'Not exactly.' Rachel made a helpless gesture. 'I just wish I'd known, that's all.'

Joe hesitated. 'But you know about the accident, right?'

'Well, I know she fell off the Johansens' yacht and hit her head,' replied Rachel at once. 'And that she apparently wasn't wearing a life jacket. I'll certainly take that up with her father, if I get the chance.' She paused. 'I don't suppose you have any idea when she'll be allowed to leave the hospital? I mean, if she's been there three days already…'

Joe stifled an oath. This was what he'd been afraid of. Evidently, his address wasn't the only thing Steve had kept from his ex-wife, and now Joe was faced with the unpleasant task of having to tell her himself or allowing her to walk into her daughter's room, totally blind to the circumstances of her condition.

He'd been silent too long and Rachel wasn't a fool. She'd noticed his expression and now she demanded, 'Why are you looking so grim?' She swallowed. 'What do you know that I don't?'

Joe blew out a breath. Steve was going to hear about this, he thought savagely. Right now, he felt like pushing the other man's teeth down his throat. It would have given him an immense amount of satisfaction, not to mention relieving a little of his own frustration.

Obviously Rachel had come here unaware of what had happened after Daisy had been helicoptered to the hospital in Palm Cove. She had no idea that Daisy's injuries had been considered too serious to be dealt with by the Emergency Room doctors and that Daisy had been transferred to a specialist neurological unit attached to the far more expensive facility patronised by the Johansens.

'Look,' he said carefully, 'First off, Daisy's going to be fine.'

'Why doesn't that reassure me?'

'But she won't be leaving hospital for a few days yet.'

'Why not?' Rachel felt the water she'd just swallowed churning around in her stomach. My God, what had really happened? What had they kept from her? She should have guessed it had been something more serious than a simple blow to the head. 'Please,' she said, unthinkingly putting a hand on his knee. 'You've got to tell me.'

Despising the inappropriate response his body was having to those soft, damp fingers clinging to his leg, Joe gently but firmly removed them. But he kept her hand between both of his as he said, 'She had to have an operation—'

'An operation!'

Rachel looked horrified and he couldn't blame her. He knew a momentary urge to comfort her, to pull her into his arms and hold her close, but he determinedly suppressed it. He knew where that could lead.

'It was just a small operation,' he said, smoothing her knuckles with his thumb. 'There was some pressure and it had to be relieved. But as I say, she's making great progress.'

Rachel was trembling. He could feel it. The hand he was holding was shaking uncontrollably and, abandoning any hope of remaining objective, Joe slipped his hand around her neck and pulled her towards him.

She didn't resist, probably because she was too shocked to notice what was happening. She pressed her hot face into the hollow of his throat and, seconds later, he felt her tears soaking the front of his shirt.

'God, Rachel,' he muttered, his hands tightening automatically, and then Luther turned and saw them.

The chauffeur knew better than to show any emotion, but Joe realised that during the upheaval of the last few minutes they had reached their destination. The rather tawdry blue-painted facade of the *Park Plaza* hotel was visible just across the intersection and Luther was waiting for further instructions.

With some reluctance, Joe withdrew his arms and, allowing her to rest against the supple upholstery, he lowered the screen an inch or two to speak to the other man. 'Let's go straight to the hospital, Luther,' he said briskly, and the chauffeur didn't demur.

Rachel had found a tissue in her handbag and was engrossed in repairing the damage caused by her tears. She didn't meet Joe's eyes, but he knew she was as aware of what had almost happened as he was. If Luther hadn't turned at that moment, Joe knew he wouldn't have been able to stop himself from kissing her. And that would have been a totally unforgiveable thing to do. Damn it, she needed support, not seduction.

He scowled. He didn't know what the hell was wrong with him. She was *so* not his type. He'd always gone for sophisticated women before; women who, like him, knew the score. Not inexperienced females with one failed relationship behind them and more baggage than he cared to consider.

Yet, when he looked at Rachel, he didn't see a woman who was older than he was and who already had a child. He saw a warm, vulnerable female who, he had to admit, got to him in a way none of his other girlfriends ever had. Sitting there in her travel-stained trousers and creased shirt, her heat-dampened blonde hair spilling untidily about her shoulders, she aroused emotions he would have sworn he didn't possess.

He stifled a groan. Now was so not the time to be having these kind of thoughts. Raking a hand over his own hair, he gripped the back of his neck with a tormented hand. He could feel the tension in his muscles, the tautness in his spine. And knew if he could get his hands on Steve at that moment…

But he couldn't. And he had to deal with it. Even if the kind of temptation Rachel presented drove him crazy in the process.

CHAPTER EIGHT

WHEN the car started moving again, Rachel realised that they weren't turning into the forecourt of the *Park Plaza* hotel.

She'd glimpsed the facade of the building across the intersection as she'd dried her eyes, and had assumed Luther was just waiting for the traffic signals to change in their favour before he made his move. But when the vehicle started away it ignored the entrance to the hotel, continuing down the thoroughfare they'd been travelling on before.

'But, wasn't that—?' she began, only to have Joe interrupt her.

'I thought you might prefer to go straight to the hospital,' he said, settling back beside her. 'I know Daisy's eager to see you.'

'Is she?' Tears pricked Rachel's eyes again, but she determinedly blinked them away. She'd already made a fool of herself by breaking down in front of him. She just hoped he didn't think she was putting on an act for his benefit. 'So—so how serious was this operation?'

Joe blew out a sigh. 'Fairly serious,' he said, after a moment. 'As I said before, there was some pressure on her brain and it had to be relieved.'

Rachel couldn't prevent her gasp of horror. 'My God! No wonder Steve was so reluctant to let me know what had happened.'

'Yeah, well.' Joe tried to be pragmatic. 'It's possible he

wanted to wait until she'd had the operation before he called you. Until the crisis was over, so to speak.'

'You think?'

Rachel looked at him with rain-washed green eyes and Joe knew he couldn't lie to her. 'Okay, maybe not,' he conceded. 'I guess he didn't want to admit he'd screwed up. All I can say in his defence is that as soon as it was realised that she needed specialist treatment he had her transferred to a neurological unit that's used to dealing with head injuries.'

Rachel's eyes widened. 'So she's not at the hospital near the *Park Plaza*?'

'She's at another facility in the town,' he explained evenly. 'She's had the best treatment money can buy, I can vouch for that.'

Rachel caught her lower lip between her teeth. 'I booked into the *Park Plaza* hotel because it was near the hospital,' she murmured, half to herself. And then, realising he was listening to her, she said quickly, 'How much further do we have to go?'

'Not far.' Joe had to suppress the urge to take her in his arms again. He couldn't forget that, if he hadn't gone to meet her at the airport, she'd still be totally in the dark. He saw the white walls of the Steinberg Clinic ahead of them and moved forward again to speak to the chauffeur. 'Pull under the portico, will you, Luther? Then, after you've dropped us off, find somewhere to park, okay?'

'Yes, sir.'

Despite the fact that Rachel had the car door open before either Luther or his employer could forestall her, the two men both came to offer their assistance. 'I can manage, thanks,' she insisted tensely, but this time Joe didn't hesitate before gripping her wrist.

'I'm coming with you,' he said, and they walked through the automatic glass doors into the clinic together. 'Humour me. I'm familiar with the form here. You're not.'

Although Rachel wanted to object, it turned out she was grateful for his presence after all. There was an armed security guard just inside the doors who might well have questioned her identity, and a glamorous receptionist manning the desk who was unlike any hospital receptionist she had ever seen before.

Happily they both recognised Joe, and after some embarrassing affectation on behalf of the receptionist, they were instantly allowed to enter the lift, which was controlled by yet another security guard.

Rachel looked up at Joe as the lift ascended, aware she'd been something less than appreciative of his help. 'Thanks,' she said, touching his arm with a tentative finger. 'I guess I owe you one.'

A knot twisted in Joe's belly, but he managed to keep his tone light as he said, 'I'll let you know when I want to collect, shall I?' And for the first time since he'd told her about Daisy's operation a small smile tilted the corners of her far too delectable mouth.

The lift stopped at the second floor and they stepped out onto a beige-carpeted landing. A nurse's station was situated opposite, and there were swing doors giving access to the private rooms at either side of the hallway.

There were two nurses on duty when they approached, and, recognising Joe, one of them—a curvaceous redhead whose uniform bodice was open to reveal a very impressive cleavage—came to greet them. 'Have you come to see Daisy again, Mr Mendez? I hope she realises what a very lucky girl she is.'

Her eyes had flickered over his companion as she spoke, and Rachel guessed she was wondering what he was doing with someone like her. Ironically, the nurse herself was much more his type, and she'd probably decided that they'd merely shared a lift together.

'Actually, I've brought her a very special visitor,' remarked Joe drily. 'This is Daisy's mother. From England. Is it okay if we go straight in?'

'Oh!' To say the nurse was startled would have been a vast understatement. 'Oh, yes. Yes, go ahead. Dr Gonzales is on his way to see her, but I don't suppose he'll object to her mother visiting her.'

'Good.'

Joe took hold of Rachel's arm just above her elbow and guided her towards the swing doors to the right of the nurses' station. Pushing open one of the doors with his free hand, he allowed her to precede him into a discreetly lit corridor with maybe half a dozen rooms situated along its wide expanse.

Rachel noticed that all the patients' rooms seemed to be on one side of the corridor, with double doors to emergency facilities and operating theatres located opposite. It was very luxurious, very quiet, and Rachel couldn't help a twinge of anxiety that Daisy had had to be treated at such a place.

'This is Daisy's room,' murmured Joe, indicating the third door down. 'I won't come in with you. You'll appreciate a few minutes on your own.' He paused and then, with an unexpected thickening of his tone, he added, 'Don't take any notice of the way she looks. She's going to be fine, I promise.'

Rachel opened her mouth to ask what he meant. But he was already striding back towards the swing doors, and the atmosphere of the place didn't encourage raised voices. Instead, with a deep breath, she put her hand on the handle of the door and pressed down.

Daisy looked lost in the huge hospital bed, her face, what Rachel could see of it, almost as white as the pillows behind her. Rachel had been expecting bruising; what she hadn't expected was the bandage that circled Daisy's forehead, or the swelling around her eye that gave her face a lopsided appearance.

Her heart leapt into her throat and she felt the treacherous sting of tears threatening to betray her again. But she remembered what Joe had said, and the advice implicit in his words, and controlled herself. She mustn't let Daisy see how upset her appearance had made her, and stepping into the room, she said, 'Now what have you been doing with yourself?' in a soft but teasing tone.

Daisy had been lying on her side, staring out of the windows, which Rachel now saw overlooked the gardens at the back of the clinic. Lawns, flowerbeds and pleasant tree-shaded walkways provided a recreational area for patients who were well enough to go outside, and there were still one or two people enjoying the somewhat watery sunshine that had broken through the clouds.

Daisy turned her head at the sound of her mother's voice, and if Rachel had had any doubts about coming, they dissolved at that moment. Daisy's face crumpled, and she held out a trembling hand towards her mother. Rachel didn't hesitate before hurrying across the room to take it, then cupped her daughter's face with fingers that were predictably unsteady.

'Oh, Daisy,' she said, pressing her lips together briefly before bending to kiss the girl's bruised cheek. 'Baby, I'm so glad to see you.'

'Me too,' sniffed Daisy, clinging to Rachel's fingers. 'Oh, Mum, it's been so awful! They had to drill a hole in my head and they had to shave off half my hair.'

'I know, I know, darling.' Rachel struggled to hide her anxiety. 'But it sounds as if you've had the best treatment possible, and that's the important thing.'

'I don't like hospitals,' said Daisy at once, her eyes brimming with tears. 'I don't like being here. I want to go home.'

'And you will,' Rachel assured her comfortingly. 'As soon as you're feeling better.'

'I feel better now!'

'Oh, Daisy.' Rachel took a steadying breath. 'As soon as the doctor says you're fit to leave, you can. I'm sure your father and—and Lauren have been worried sick about you.'

Daisy's chin trembled. 'I haven't seen Lauren,' she said tearfully. 'Dad says she doesn't like hospitals. Or—or sick people.'

Rachel bit her tongue against the retort that sprang to her lips and, as if realising how inflammatory her words had been, Daisy added hastily, 'Dad said it's because her mother died in hospital. She had some kind of disease that attacks your liver. Cirius, or something.'

Cirrhosis, thought Rachel flatly, resisting the urge to speculate about whether Mrs Johansen had been rather more than a social drinker, and said, 'That's a shame. She can't have been very old when she died.'

'She wasn't.' Daisy was distracted from her own problems by relating the story. 'Mr Johansen misses her a lot.'

'I bet.' Rachel hesitated. 'You've been staying with him, haven't you?'

'Mmm.' Daisy attempted a nod, but it evidently pained her and she winced. 'Daddy and Lauren live with him,' she went on when she'd recovered. 'He's nice. You'll like him.'

'I doubt if I'll even meet him,' declared Rachel ruefully. 'Once you're out of hospital, you'll continue with your holiday and I'll go home.'

'No!' As Rachel would have moved to the chair beside the bed, Daisy grasped her arm. 'You can't leave,' she protested. 'I don't want you to.'

'Oh, Daisy.' Rachel could see the girl was getting distressed and she tried to reassure her. 'I can't stay here. I have to get back, you know that. Besides, what would your father say?'

'I don't care what he says,' muttered Daisy in a choked voice. 'He doesn't care about me. He only cares about Lauren.'

'Now, Daisy—'

'It's true!' she cried. 'He only wants me here because the company expects their executives to be family men, and he and Lauren can't have any children.'

'Daisy!' Rachel stared at her. 'You don't know that.'

'I do too.' Daisy groped for a tissue from the box on the bedside cabinet and Rachel put one into her hand. 'I heard them talking one night after I was supposed to be in bed.'

'Daisy!' Rachel was torn between her desire to know what her daughter had heard and the equally strong conviction that she shouldn't be listening to gossip. 'I don't think this is anything to do with me.'

'But it is!' Daisy was determined to make her point. 'You know you've always wondered why Dad suddenly started showing an interest in me.'

Rachel's jaw dropped. 'I didn't say that.'

'You didn't have to. I'm not stupid, Mum. I'm, like, thirteen, not three.'

Rachel sighed. 'All the same—'

'Ah, it's Mrs Carlyle, I believe.'

The voice came from behind her and Rachel sprang up from the bed as an elderly man in a white coat and wearing half spectacles came briskly into the room. She hoped he hadn't been listening to their conversation. If so, he must have a very poor opinion of her.

'Um—yes,' she said awkwardly, and the man smiled.

'I thought so.' He came across the room to shake her hand. 'I'm Dr Gonzales. Daisy is my patient. And I have to say she looks much brighter now than she did when I saw her this morning.'

'That's 'cos my mum's here,' said Daisy at once, and Dr Gonzales inclined his head.

'Most probably,' he agreed, consulting the chart hooked to the foot of the bed. 'But we'll see, shall we?' He looked up. 'How is your head feeling now? Do you still have some pain?'

'No.'

Daisy's response was just a little too pat and Dr Gonzales didn't look as if he was deceived. 'Maybe just a little?' suggested Rachel, remembering the way Daisy had winced earlier, and her daughter gave her a resentful look.

'You'd have some pain if someone had drilled your skull,' she countered sulkily as a nurse followed the doctor into the room. 'I'll feel better when I get out of here.' Then, as Rachel widened her eyes in warning, 'Well, I will.'

'I suggest we allow your mother to go and get a cup of coffee,' declared Dr Gonzales smoothly as the nurse began to roll back the sleeve of Daisy's gown. 'She looks a little tired, don't you think?' Then, to Rachel, 'Perhaps we could have a few words later this evening? I'd like to explain what has happened and how long I think Daisy needs to stay here.'

'Of course.' Rachel glanced at her watch. It read almost midnight, but it was still on British time. 'I—er—I need to speak to someone. To arrange about my luggage. If you could give me half an hour?'

'Take an hour,' advised Dr Gonzales kindly. 'I'll be here all evening. You might like to have a rest. Are you staying somewhere close by?'

'The *Park Plaza* hotel,' said Rachel, and she thought he seemed a little surprised by her answer. But he didn't demur.

'Shall we say eight-thirty?' he suggested. 'In my office. The receptionist will tell you where it is.'

Daisy gazed at her despairingly. 'You're not leaving?' She choked back a sob. 'I don't want you to go.'

'I'll be back.' Rachel glanced at the doctor, and he nodded his head almost imperceptibly. She squeezed Daisy's hand. 'You be good, baby. I'll be back before you've even noticed I've gone.'

There was no sign of Joe when Rachel let herself out of Daisy's room and she guessed he must be waiting downstairs. He couldn't have left, she assured herself as she took the lift down to the lobby. Her suitcase was still in the boot of the limousine.

But when the lift doors opened it was Luther who was standing there, waiting for her. 'Mr Mendez had to leave,' he explained politely. 'He sends his apologies and has instructed me to escort you to your hotel.'

'Oh.' Rachel's stomach hollowed with disappointment. Until that moment, she hadn't realised how much she'd wanted to see Joe again. 'Well, thank you.' She glanced uncomfortably at the receptionist, who was watching their exchange with obvious interest. She forced a smile. 'Shall we go?'

The limousine was visible as soon as they stepped out of the doors; its sleek black lines dominated every other vehicle on the parking lot. Luther helped her into the back, then closed the door and got behind the wheel. He moved easily for such a big man, and the smile he gave her through the rear-view mirror was reassuring.

'The *Park Plaza*, right?' he said, and Rachel nodded.

Then, before the screen between them could be raised, she shifted forward in her seat and said nervously, 'Exactly how far away is it? Could I walk from the hotel to the hospital?'

'Not a good idea,' declared Luther without hesitation. 'I guess it's over a mile, and most people hire a car to get around.' He paused. 'That's not your problem. Mr Mendez is letting you have the use of one of his cars while you're here.'

Rachel's lips parted. 'But—he can't do that.'

'Hey, you don't tell Mr Mendez he can't do nothing.' Luther grinned. 'Leastways, not when he's just thinking of your safety. You're a stranger, Ms Carlyle. You don't know the area. It can be a dangerous place, especially at night.'

Rachel shook her head. 'I don't know what to say.'

'Don't say nothing.' Luther was dismissive. 'You just tell Mr Mendez how you feel when you see him again.'

When you see him again.

Considering how Rachel had been feeling about Joe Mendez when she'd landed in Miami, it was amazing how reassuring those words sounded. Did Joe intend to see her again or did Luther mean he might run into her at the hospital? Either way, the prospect was massively—and dangerously—appealing.

CHAPTER NINE

JOE stood at the windows of his condo, looking out at the angry waves crashing against the shore. Although the rain had gone, the wind had picked up in its absence, bending the palms that lined Ocean Drive, and causing the few pedestrians to stay out of reach of the blowing sand.

It was almost dark, and he hadn't even started to get ready for the reception he was due to attend in South Beach. The painter son of one of Macrosystems' directors was having his first showing in one of the art deco galleries on Lenox Avenue, and Joe had accepted an invitation more out of respect for the father than the son.

Of course, when he'd first heard about the showing, he hadn't had any inkling that other matters might be occupying his mind—or that the woman he'd tried his damnedest to forget would have come back into his life. How could he have known that Daisy would have an accident so serious that her father would have to contact her mother? And why, when he'd learned that Steve was making no arrangements to meet his ex-wife, had he decided to get involved? Rachel wasn't his concern, damn it. So why did he feel as if she was?

It was time he put the Carlyles and their problems behind him. For this evening, at least. Tomorrow, he intended to speak to Steve and find out why the hell he hadn't been honest with Daisy's mother. He'd have allowed his ex-wife to arrive in Miami without even knowing where her daughter was being treated.

But it still wasn't his problem, he reminded himself irritably, turning away from the windows and surveying the lamplit room behind him. Pale wood and terracotta-coloured furnishings gave the huge room a stark simplicity, the space maximised by carefully chosen articles of furniture that offered comfort without dwarfing their surroundings.

The penthouse living space had windows on two sides, and leather-seated chairs surrounding an Italian marble-topped table occupied the other embrasure. It provided an intimate dining area, useful when his guests were small in number, but this evening he found no pleasure in his possessions. He was impatient and on edge, unsure why he hadn't waited at the hospital. He'd wanted to, God knew, but things were getting far too heavy. He'd always been in command of his relationships before, but where Rachel was concerned it was a whole new ball game.

And he didn't like it.

The sound of the intercom penetrated his grim introspection, and seconds later his housekeeper came to ask if he was at home to a Mr Carlyle.

'You did say *Mr* Carlyle?' he asked sharply, and in spite of what he'd been telling himself just a moment ago the idea that Rachel might have found out where he lived caused his blood to pump hotly through his veins. After all, Marla was Mexican, and her English wasn't always perfect.

'Mr Carlyle, yes,' she repeated, her brown eyes bright with enquiry. 'You will see him, yes?'

Joe glanced at his watch. He had precisely forty minutes before he was due at the gallery. A quick shower—he ran his hands over the stubble on his jawline and decided he could do without a shave—and a clean shirt and trousers and he would be ready. At least people didn't dress up for these occasions. There'd be punks there in tie-dyed tee shirts and shorts.

'Okay,' he said now. He'd welcome the chance to tell Steve how he felt about the way he'd treated Rachel. Though maybe not tonight, he mused, revising his opinion. It might look as if he had a personal interest.

'Yes, sir.'

Marla departed to let Steve in, and Joe walked across to the bar to help himself to a Scotch over ice. He grimaced. Charles always said that he ruined a perfectly good whisky that way, but Charles wasn't here, and that was the way his father always took it.

There were voices in the foyer—women's voices, he realised—and he felt a surge of irritation when Marla showed both Steve and Lauren Carlyle into the room. Had Steve brought his wife deliberately, hoping Joe wouldn't say anything controversial if Lauren was present? Their friendship had been sorely tested recently, what with the lies Steve had told about his age and Joe's suspicion that Rachel was not the manipulative bitch her ex-husband had always claimed.

'Hey, Joe!' Steve came into the room with an air of phony confidence, holding out his hand towards the other man as if certain of his welcome despite Joe's expression. 'How are you?'

Joe shook hands with some reluctance, accepting the kiss Lauren bestowed on either cheek without response. Her hands clutched his arms, and she took the opportunity to press her scantily clad breasts against his chest as she did so. It wasn't the first time she'd come on to him in this way, and he was well aware of what she was trying to do.

He wondered fleetingly if Steve had put her up to it. Was he prepared to turn a blind eye to Lauren's indiscretions if it ensured his advancement at Mendez Macrosystems? It was a cynical thought, and one Joe wouldn't have considered a couple of weeks ago. But meeting Rachel and Daisy had changed his opinion of Steve's character.

'I hope you don't mind us turning up like this,' Steve was saying now as Lauren returned to slide a sinuous hand under her husband's arm. 'I just wanted to thank you for meeting Rachel at the airport.'

Joe swallowed a mouthful of his Scotch before saying, 'How did you know I went to the airport?' He crossed to the bar to refresh his drink and held up his glass enquiringly.

'Oh.' Steve's colour had deepened a little. 'Nothing for me, thanks.' Then, after Lauren had asked for a glass of white wine, he continued, 'Bill Napier told me where you were. I'd heard you were in the office today, and I wanted to tell you how much I appreciate you visiting Daisy.' He pulled a wry face. 'When I heard you'd gone to pick up Rachel, I had to come and thank you. I mean, it's not as if she needed to make the trip.'

'You don't think so?'

Joe handed Lauren her wine and regarded the other man over the rim of his glass. Sensing some tension here, Lauren said quickly, 'What Steve means is that Rachel has never trusted us to look after Daisy properly. You can't imagine how galling that is, particularly as he's been denied a father's rights for years.'

Joe arched a quizzical brow. 'Daisy did have an accident,' he reminded her, and Lauren met his gaze with an appealing look.

'You're surely not blaming Steve for that?' she protested in a little-girl voice, pouting in a way Joe was sure achieved positive results with her husband. Though not, unfortunately, with him. 'The girl is so clumsy. Anyone can see that. If she wasn't so fat, she might have been able to save herself.'

'Lauren!' Even Steve seemed to realise she'd gone too far, and Lauren widened her eyes indignantly.

'You said that too,' she accused sulkily. 'You said she was just like her mother.'

'Lauren!' Steve spoke again, and this time there was no mistaking the anger in his voice. 'I don't think this is the time to be discussing whether Daisy's fat or not. We came to thank Joe for visiting her. You know better than anyone that it's no fun spending time in a hospital.'

'Oh, that's so true.'

Lauren shuddered dramatically, and Joe's brows rose in surprise. 'I didn't know you'd been in hospital, Lauren,' he said politely. 'I hope it was nothing serious.'

'Lauren's not been ill,' said Steve swiftly. 'She's talking about when her mother was dying and she had to visit her every day.' He put an arm about his wife's shoulders. 'She had such a tough time. She and her father both did.'

Not to mention the late Mrs Johansen, thought Joe drily, wondering why he'd never noticed these flaws in Steve's make-up before. It was as if he was seeing a whole new person, one he didn't particularly like.

'Anyway, I guess you told Rachel where Daisy is being treated,' went on Steve conversationally. 'Knowing her, she'll probably spend all her time at the clinic. Still, it'll give me a break. Trying to keep a kid of thirteen entertained is no joke.'

Joe's brows ascended again. 'You've been spending a lot of time at the clinic?' he queried mildly. 'I didn't realise that.'

Steve pulled a sheepish face. 'Some,' he said, looking a little defensive. 'But you know how it is. I'm no good in the sick room. And looking at Daisy's face just makes me feel sick.'

Joe knew an almost uncontrollable urge to hit him. 'I don't suppose it's much fun for Daisy either,' he retorted, unable to hide the irritation in his voice. 'For God's sake, Steve, she's your daughter! And if you're not exactly responsible for what happened to her, you can't deny you were supposed to be looking out for her when the accident occurred.'

Steve looked indignant now, and Lauren squeezed his arm before giving Joe a reproachful look. 'You didn't mean that, did you, Joe?' she said in a baby voice. 'Steve loves his daughter. He can't help it if Daisy's injuries make him squeamish.'

'Of course he can help it!' Joe was angry now. 'Daisy's injuries will heal, please God, no thanks to him. But what irritates me is the way the two of you seem to have absolved yourselves of all responsibility for what happened. If I didn't know better, I'd have thought you'd informed Rachel of the accident just so she'd take up the slack.'

'It wasn't our fault,' protested Steve, sounding resentful. 'It's all right for you, Joe. You swan into the clinic whenever you feel like it and you know that the staff will fall over themselves to lick your boots. Me, I'm just Daisy's father. They tolerate my presence and that's about it.'

'Perhaps if you spent more time with Daisy they'd have more respect for you,' said Joe harshly. 'As I understand it, you've only visited the kid a couple of times since she had the operation.'

'Three times,' said Steve sharply, as if that let him off the hook. 'And as soon as she's out of there, we'll take her to Disney World.'

Joe rolled his eyes. 'She won't want trips to Disney World,' he snapped in exasperation. 'What she'll need is a little rest and relaxation when she's discharged. Personally, I'd suggest you take a couple of weeks off work and spend time with her. Talk to her, find out what she's been doing since you last saw her. Show her you're her father in more than just name.'

'Oh, but Steve and I are going to New York next weekend!' exclaimed Lauren at once. 'Isn't that right, babe?' She looked up at her husband. 'Daisy's only staying for another week and then she's going home.'

'Daisy won't be flying back to England any time soon,' said Joe finally. He slammed his glass back onto the bar. 'Have you given any thought to Rachel's feelings at all?'

'Rachel?'

Lauren looked nonplussed, and even Steve appeared taken aback by the non sequitur.

'Yeah, Rachel,' said Joe shortly, half wishing he hadn't brought her name up. 'When were you planning to tell her how serious Daisy's injuries were? Damn it, she didn't even know she'd been moved to a specialist facility.'

Steve scowled. 'She'd have found out soon enough,' he muttered, staring down at the Chinese rug beneath his feet. But when he lifted his head and met Joe's accusing gaze, his expression shifted. 'What's it to you? What has she been telling you about me? Was it my fault she was out with some guy the night I called?'

Joe's jaw tightened. Was that true? Had Rachel been spending the evening—night?—with another man when Steve had tried to ring her? He felt a tightening in his gut that had nothing to do with Daisy and everything to do with her mother. Was that why she'd got only half the story? Was he jumping in with both feet when he'd only got half the story too?

'I suggest we say no more about it,' he declared flatly. 'As you say, it's really nothing to do with me. My only concern is that Daisy gets the best treatment possible.'

'Hey, that's my concern too!' exclaimed Steve, his tone indicating some relief at Joe's capitulation. 'And we'd better be making a move. I want to visit Daisy before her mother can poison her mind against me again.'

Rachel's room at the *Park Plaza* hotel was hardly a five-star accommodation. But it was clean and the bed was reasonably comfortable. So much so that, when Luther dropped her off, she was grateful just to flop down onto it and close her eyes.

She was so tired. Her body didn't care what time the clock said; she'd flown the Atlantic and she felt utterly exhausted. Finding out that Daisy's injuries were more serious than she'd been told hadn't helped either. Without Joe's support and guidance, she'd have been whistling in the wind.

She refused to consider what meeting Joe again had meant to her. She'd been so sure that if they did meet again she'd be able to handle it. But she was afraid she was beginning to rely on him more and more. And that was stupid. Joe Mendez was not a man a woman like her could depend on, and she was fooling herself if she thought he found her anything more than a minor distraction.

It had been dark outside when she'd closed her eyes, but when she opened them again the room was filled with sunlight. Scrambling up, she managed to bring her watch into focus, her breath catching when she saw the time. Not that she needed the watch to tell her it was morning. She'd slept for twelve hours straight, still dressed in the shirt and trousers she'd worn to travel in.

Her head throbbing now, she glanced round and saw her suitcase standing just inside the door where the porter had left it. Swinging it up onto the crumpled coverlet, she found the key in her bag and hastily unlocked it.

Seeing the clean clothes laid out inside reminded her that she hadn't had a shower for two days. She felt hot and grubby, the air conditioner making only half-hearted inroads into the room's humidity. Stripping off her clothes, she padded barefoot into the adjoining bathroom and turned on the shower.

Fifteen minutes later, she felt infinitely cleaner and brighter, and rummaging in her case, she brought out navy linen shorts and a pink tank top. There was no hairdryer, but it was so hot she knew her hair would dry naturally. Then, content she wouldn't embarrass her daughter, she grabbed her bag and left the room.

Daisy had been on her mind ever since she'd opened her eyes. She hadn't forgotten that she'd promised to go back the previous evening, and aside from Daisy's distress she'd let Dr

Gonzales down, too. She was also desperate for a drink. She'd had nothing since the bottle of water Joe had given her in the car, and she was sure her headache was partly due to dehydration.

Thankfully, there was a coffee shop and a small pharmacy attached to the hotel, and she was able to buy herself a coffee to go and some chocolates for Daisy. Normally she wouldn't encourage her to eat rich confectionery, but these were exceptional circumstances. Then, sipping the coffee, she went outside to look for a taxi.

There was no taxi in sight, but she refused to consider what Luther had said about Joe lending her a car. And luckily, a taxi arrived soon afterwards. The driver offloaded two passengers and their luggage and she was able to grab it. 'The Steinberg Clinic, please,' she said, sinking into the back seat.

It was after nine o'clock when she got to the clinic, and she stowed the half-drunk styrofoam mug of coffee in a waste bin before going in. As luck would have it, a young man was manning the desk this morning, and after she'd identified herself he had no problem in directing her to the second floor.

She was aware of the security guard watching her as she took the lift, but she reached the second floor without incident. She had to identify herself again at the nurses' station and then she was allowed to make her way to Daisy's room. But when she opened the door, she discovered Daisy already had a visitor.

Joe Mendez was lounging on the wide windowsill beside her daughter's bed, and Daisy was giggling at something he'd said. There was such an air of camaraderie between them that Rachel almost felt as if she was intruding. Yet she was glad Daisy wasn't on her own, she told herself. Even if she'd never expected to see Joe again.

Joe got up from the sill as Rachel stepped into the room, and Daisy, sensing another presence, turned her head. 'Mum!' she exclaimed eagerly. And then, as if remembering Rachel had promised to come back the night before and hadn't, her expression changed. 'I thought you'd forgotten I was here.'

'Oh, Daisy!' Rachel rolled her lips inward, pressing the box of chocolates to her chest like a shield. 'I fell asleep,' she admitted honestly, uncomfortably aware that Joe was listening. Then, turning to him, 'Um—thanks for visiting Daisy again, Mr Mendez. It's very kind of you.'

Joe tucked his palms into the back pockets of his trousers and swayed back on his heels before replying. He was formally dressed this morning, his pin-striped grey shirt and charcoal-grey trousers indicating a business meeting. 'I was passing,' he said. Then, his eyes darkening, 'Did you sleep well?'

'Too well,' murmured Rachel, feeling the heat rising up her throat as he continued to look at her. Were her breasts puckering? she wondered. Was the film of perspiration she could feel breaking out all over her visible? She lifted her hand and made a futile attempt to fan herself. 'It's very hot.'

'It's Miami in August,' remarked Joe drily, but Rachel noticed it didn't seem to bother him. He looked so cool—and gorgeous, she thought, looking away before he noticed the effect he was having on her. Dear heaven, she was behaving like a schoolgirl. She had to stop reacting in this way.

'Mr Mendez comes most days,' put in Daisy, apparently deciding she'd been ignored long enough. She fumbled for something half-hidden beneath the coverlet. 'Look what he's brought me.'

She produced something that looked like the iPod Rachel had bought her at Christmas. But it was smaller and slimmer, and when Daisy touched a switch a small screen flickered to life. 'It's a video iPod,' she said proudly. 'Isn't it great? I can download videos as well as music and watch them on the screen.'

'Really?' Rachel was impressed in spite of herself, but there was no way she could allow her daughter to accept such an expensive gift from him. She licked her lips and turned to

Joe again. 'It's very nice,' she said inadequately, 'But Daisy can't keep it.'

'Mum!'

Daisy's cry of protest was predictable, but Rachel couldn't help that. 'It's too much,' she said, avoiding Joe's dark gaze. 'I'm sorry.'

'But Mum…'

Daisy was getting tearful now, and Joe felt a surge of impatience as Rachel held her ground. He'd wanted to do this for Daisy; wanted to give her something to make her time in hospital more fun. And give him an excuse to visit her again, he admitted ruefully. Because, now that Rachel was here, he definitely wanted to see her again, whatever excuse he had to make.

'Mum, you can't stop me from having it,' Daisy was saying sulkily. 'It's mine, not yours. Mr Mendez has already downloaded a load of teen movies, so I'm not bored while I'm lying here.'

'I'm sorry,' Rachel muttered, but now she couldn't prevent her gaze from shifting to Joe's dark face. He should have known better, she thought crossly. He hardly knew the child.

'How about if Daisy only borrows it while she's in the hospital?' he suggested mildly. 'I don't mind. I've got a stack of them lying around the place. It's no big deal.'

Not for you, maybe, Rachel brooded, aware she was fighting a losing battle. Joe was determined to win this argument and she was fairly sure there was humour lurking behind his eyes. He was probably enjoying her confusion. Another anecdote to regale her ex-husband with perhaps?

'Please, Mum.' Now that she saw a glimmer of hope on the horizon, Daisy was prepared to be docile. With an appealing smile, she added, 'Are those chocolates for me?'

'What?' Rachel became aware that she was practically squashing the box of chocolates to her chest. 'Oh, yes.' With a hurried gesture, she handed the box over. 'Sorry. They may be a bit soft.'

'Unlike the giver,' murmured Joe, crossing the room and dropping the mocking remark in her ear. Then, turning back, 'Bye, Daisy. I guess I'll see you *both* later.'

CHAPTER TEN

'THANKS, Mr Mendez.'

Daisy evidently thought the controversy was over, but as Joe closed the door behind him Rachel knew she wasn't prepared to leave it like that. 'I won't be a minute,' she said to her startled daughter, and jerking open the door again, she stepped into the corridor outside.

'Mr Mendez!'

Closing Daisy's door, she called his name, and Joe, who had almost reached the double doors into the reception area, paused at once. Turning, he saw her, and Rachel couldn't deny a ridiculous sense of satisfaction when he strolled back to her.

'Hi,' he said, as if they hadn't just been involved in a dispute in Daisy's room. 'What can I do for you?'

Rachel pressed the palms of her hands together, not knowing how she was going to handle this. 'I wish you hadn't given Daisy such an expensive present,' she said at last, and Joe's mouth took on a cynical twist.

'Well, hey, and I thought you were going to thank me for loaning you that automobile,' he remarked drily, hands on his hips. 'I should have known better.'

Rachel sighed. 'I don't know anything about an automobile,' she said, ignoring what Luther had told her. 'And you're deliberately confusing me...'

'Am I?' He didn't sound concerned. 'So?'

'So...' Rachel glanced up into his disturbing face, wishing she had more experience in these matters. These days all her knowledge of men seemed to come from books she'd written or read, and she couldn't manipulate Joe Mendez like she could one of her characters. 'I—er—I'd like your word that you won't turn Daisy's head with any more extravagant gifts. She's an impressionable teenager, and although we're not poor by any means, I can't afford to spend hundreds of pounds—dollars—every time she sees something she wants.'

A muscle in Joe's jaw jerked spasmodically. 'You don't pull your punches, do you, Ms Carlyle?' he said coldly. 'Believe it or not, I didn't give Daisy the video iPod with any intention of turning her head or encouraging her to believe that she can get anything she wants without working for it.'

'No?'

It was obvious Rachel didn't believe him, and Joe felt compelled to go on. 'No,' he said flatly. 'I don't care what you believe, but I haven't always been in the happy position of being able to afford anything that takes my fancy either. Growing up, my family was like yours, except we were immigrants. I didn't go short, but I always knew I'd have to work if I wanted to make a success of my life.'

Rachel stared at him. 'But your family owns a multi-million-dollar company,' she protested, and Joe gave an angry snort.

'Yeah, they do now,' he conceded. 'My father was fortunate enough to understand computers, and between us we found a way to use macro technology to simplify disciplines in science and economics. We were lucky. Our idea took off. But that was only ten years ago, after I left Harvard.'

'Harvard!' Rachel's eyes widened and Joe pulled a wry face.

'Yeah, Harvard,' he agreed. 'What can I tell you? I was a bright student. A guy can get sponsorship if he's clever enough.'

'And you were? Clever enough, I mean?'

'No.' Joe found he couldn't lie to her, even if his answer caused her to give him a cynical look. 'Actually, my grandparents supported me.' He grimaced. 'That part was easy. Staying there wasn't.'

'Oh, well…' Rachel shrugged. 'It's nothing to do with me, is it?'

'No, it's not.' Joe's voice was terse and she could sense he was impatient. 'But you've made it a bone of contention between us and I'm entitled to defend myself.' He raked a hand through his short hair, causing it to spike on top of his head. 'Damn it, I don't know why we're having this conversation. It's obvious you don't believe a single word I've said.'

Rachel blinked. 'I didn't say I didn't believe you.'

'You didn't have to.' His voice was harsh. 'God, why do I let you get under my skin?'

Rachel swallowed. The corridor seemed very empty suddenly. 'I didn't know I did,' she protested, feeling the flesh on her arms prickle with anticipation, and he scowled.

'Well, you do,' he told her roughly, and she thought he was going to turn and stride back the way he'd come. But instead he reached for her, pulling her in closer so he could cover her mouth with his.

Desire came hot and fast, her bones melting as his hungry tongue thrust into her mouth. His hands gripped her hips, jerking her against him, and the hardness of his body was unmistakeable.

Joe groaned. This wasn't meant to have happened. He'd spent over a week—and all of last night, incidentally—telling himself that he'd imagined the effect she had on him. He'd known women before, plenty of them, and he'd always been able to walk away without looking back. For God's sake, he hadn't even slept with Rachel, yet he hungered for her with a need that defied description.

There was something about her that made the blood run hot in his veins and caused a wholly carnal reaction in his groin.

For heaven's sake, he'd been half-aroused since she'd walked into Daisy's room in those so-conservative shorts that nonetheless displayed the sexy length of her legs.

He'd wanted to touch her then, to run his fingers up the insides of her thighs and discover for himself if she was as aroused as he was. He'd wanted to bury his face between her breasts and lick the beads of sweat from her delectable cleavage.

His hands slid around her, finding the curve of her spine, the provocative separation of her bottom. He moulded her to him, her softness a delicious counterpoint to his hardness, and knew that, whatever happened, he was going to see her again.

With her nipples probing the fine silk of his shirt, it was hard to let her go. But he had to. Dragging his mouth from hers, he ran his thumb over her bottom lip with an urgency that revealed his raw frustration.

'I've got to go,' he said harshly. 'But I want to see you again.'

Rachel swayed a little as he spoke. It was an effort to think coherently when her head was swimming, and the knowledge that once again he had the advantage was causing goose bumps to feather her skin.

But she couldn't let him see how shaken she was, and with a determined effort she said, 'I suppose you're bound to see me again when you come to visit Daisy,' as if that thought didn't fill her with panic. 'I'd better get back—'

'Wait!' Once again, Joe's hand captured her arm. 'I mean I want to see *you* again.' He paused. 'Have dinner with me. Tonight.'

'I can't.'

It was an instinctive denial born of a need to protect herself, but Joe wouldn't accept it. 'Why can't you?' he demanded. 'You're not seeing Steve, are you?'

'Steve?' Rachel looked astounded. 'Heavens, no.'

'So maybe you feel some loyalty to this guy you're seeing back home?' he suggested, feeling his stomach clench at the thought.

But Rachel only shook her head. 'Paul's a friend, that's all,' she said firmly.

As if Joe was something more than that!

'Okay, then...'

'There's Daisy to consider,' she said, realising belatedly that she could have used Paul as an excuse.

'Does that mean, if you didn't have Daisy to consider, you'd have no objections?' he queried, and when she didn't respond, 'They settle Daisy down for the night before nine o'clock. I could pick you up outside.'

Rachel sighed. 'Why?'

'Why?' Joe's hand fell to his side. 'You need to ask?' His eyes were suddenly dark and intense. 'Rachel, you know why.'

She shifted uneasily. 'I can't believe there isn't some other woman waiting for you to ask her out.'

Joe scowled. 'Okay, maybe I would have no difficulty in getting a date for this evening, but I don't want anyone else, I want you.'

Rachel bit her lip. 'If you feel guilty about what happened just now,' she began and Joe uttered a strangled oath.

'I don't feel guilty!' he snarled, wondering if he'd ever had to beg for a date before. 'I just want to spend time with someone who doesn't care about getting their picture in the papers or how much money I have in the bank. But okay, yeah, I want to sleep with you. And despite your reaction, I think you want to sleep with me.'

Rachel took a step backward. 'And you assume I'll go out with you after that?'

'Why not?' Joe's eyes rested sensually on her mouth. 'Come on, Rachel. Live dangerously for once. I've read one of your books, and I know your heroines don't get freaked out when a man tells them he's attracted to them.'

'My heroes don't expect sex on a first date,' she retorted indignantly, and Joe spread his hands in a gesture of defeat.

'Okay,' he said. 'Just dinner, then. How's that? I promise I won't try to jump you in the restaurant.'

Rachel shook her head. The temptation to do as he said and live dangerously was strong, but for the last few years she'd avoided any kind of emotional entanglement. She had no intention of allowing herself to be hurt again, and something told her any pain Joe inflicted would not be easily repaired.

Still…

'Just dinner?' She lifted her head, and Joe made a sign of assent. 'All right,' she said. 'But I have to warn you, I didn't bring any special clothes with me.'

Joe's grin was smug. 'Come as you are,' he said drily. 'Nine o'clock downstairs, right?'

Rachel's tongue circled her lower lip. 'Right.'

'Good.' Joe's voice was husky, and before she could stop him he'd wiped her lip with his finger and brought the moisture he'd collected to his lips.

Daisy wasn't very impressed when Rachel recovered herself sufficiently to enter her daughter's room again. 'What have you been doing?' she grumbled. 'I thought you came to see me, not spend time arguing with Mr Mendez.'

Arguing? Rachel felt a hysterical desire to laugh. 'Oh, it was nothing important,' she said. 'And you needn't worry, you can keep the video iPod as long as you're in here.'

'Yes.' Daisy made a fist, but then she sobered. 'Come and sit down.' She patted the bed beside her. 'I have something to tell you.'

Rachel was wary, but she seated herself on the side of Daisy's bed. 'What?'

Daisy offered her a chocolate from the box before saying, 'Dad and Lauren came to see me last night.'

'They did?' Rachel refused the chocolate before adding, 'It's just as well I didn't come back, then, isn't it?'

'Well, no, actually.' Daisy popped the rejected chocolate into her mouth. 'I think he expected you to be here.' She paused again, examining the contents of the box. 'I think that's why he brought Lauren.'

'Really?' Rachel realised that, apart from caring about Steve's treatment of Daisy, she couldn't care less about him or Lauren. 'I thought you said she didn't like hospitals.'

'She doesn't.' Daisy shrugged. 'Maybe she didn't trust Dad to be alone with you.'

'Oh, please.' Rachel stared at her. 'I don't think that's likely, do you?'

'You never know.' Daisy regarded her critically for a moment. 'You've changed, Mum. You look really pretty these days. If you could just get used to wearing more trendy gear, I think you'd be surprised at how good you look.'

'Gee, thanks.' Rachel didn't know what to say. She couldn't remember the last time someone had paid her such a nice compliment. Except when Joe had said she was beautiful, of course. But he'd had his own reasons for saying that.

'Anyway…' Rachel was eager to leave the subject of her appearance. 'How are you feeling this morning?' She studied the girl's face intently. 'You know, I do believe the swelling round your eye is going down.'

Daisy pulled a face. 'I still look like Frankenstein's sister,' she grumbled. 'Dr Gonzales says I've been very lucky, but I don't know. Do you think my face will ever look normal again?'

'Of course it will.' Rachel was optimistic. 'And you always look good to me, baby.' She sighed. 'Which reminds me, I didn't get to speak to Dr Gonzales last night, either. I hope he'll forgive me for wasting his time.'

'Gonzales is okay, I guess.' Daisy was resigned.

'Well, Joe—Mr Mendez, that is—thinks so. When he told

me you'd had to have an operation, he assured me you'd received the best treatment there is.'

Daisy frowned then. 'But Dad had already told you that, hadn't he?'

Rachel stifled a groan. 'He said you'd had an accident,' she said, prevaricating. 'I dare say he didn't want to worry me.'

Daisy didn't look as if she believed her. 'Anyway,' she said, 'when you do talk to Dr Gonzales, could you ask him when I can get out of here and go home?'

Rachel considered. 'Well, I should think that's up to your father,' she said. 'You've still got a week of your holiday left.'

Daisy pouted. 'But I don't want to finish my holiday,' she protested. 'I want to go home. Back to England. With you.'

'Oh, Daisy…' This was an eventuality Rachel hadn't anticipated. 'I don't know whether you'll be allowed to fly straight after a— Well, after an operation.' She tucked a strand of Daisy's hair behind her ear and drew back. 'Besides, your father will want you to stay.'

'You think?' Daisy spoke surprisingly cynically for a girl of her age. 'Now that he's done his duty, I don't think he can wait to get rid of me. I know Lauren can't.'

'Daisy!'

'Well, it's true. They were talking about going to New York next weekend, and I'm not included in that.'

Rachel bit her lip. 'Well, let me talk to Dr Gonzales.' *And your father*, she thought grimly. 'Then I'll let you know what he says, right?'

'All right.' Daisy managed a small smile. 'I do love you, Mum.'

'And I love you,' said Rachel fiercely as a nurse came into the room. She got to her feet. 'Now, I'll go and see if I can get some answers.'

As it turned out, Dr Gonzales wasn't available to speak to her that day. One of the nurses explained that he also worked at one of the hospitals in Miami itself, and unless there was an emergency he wouldn't be in until the following day.

There was no way Rachel could class Daisy's sudden desire to leave the hospital as an emergency, and she had the unenviable task of explaining to her daughter that Dr Gonzales' world didn't revolve around her.

Daisy complained, naturally, and she got herself into such a state that the nurse who came to check on her suggested Rachel should go and get some lunch and let Daisy have a rest. 'There's a coffee bar downstairs,' she said pleasantly. 'It will do you both good to have a break.'

The coffee bar was almost empty, and Rachel helped herself to a ham sandwich before ordering another coffee. Then, carrying her tray to a window table overlooking the forecourt of the clinic, she made an effort to eat. She should have been hungry, but so much had happened since her arrival she had little appetite.

Still, the sandwich was delicious, and after a few mouthfuls she realised she was hungry after all. She finished it and was enjoying sipping her coffee when someone sat down at her table. It was a man, and she was about to pick up her coffee and find somewhere else to sit when she realised it was Steve.

Looking at him, she thought she could forgive herself for not recognising him straight away. He'd lost weight and his skin was deeply tanned. He should have looked fit and healthy, but he didn't, and she wondered if living with Lauren wasn't quite the sinecure he'd imagined it would be.

'Hi,' he said flatly. 'Daisy said I'd find you here.' His eyes appraised her with surprising interest. 'How are you? You look—good. Different, but good.'

'Compliments from you?' Rachel was sardonic 'Gee, I wonder why?'

Steve's jaw jutted. 'Don't be like that, Rache. I'm just trying to be friendly. There's no point in you and me falling out with one another, is there?'

'Isn't there?' Rachel's look was incredulous. 'You don't think keeping the truth about Daisy's injuries from me was a little thoughtless?' She shook her head. 'Not to say downright deceitful.'

Steve scowled. 'You don't think that the way you're reacting now is why I didn't tell you?' he countered. 'I knew you'd panic. You always do.'

'I don't panic!' exclaimed Rachel defensively. 'But I was worried. And I had a right to know.'

'Why?' Steve looked sulky now, much like Daisy did when things were not going her way. 'So you can get the custody order changed?'

'No.'

'That's what you said,' Steve reminded her. 'You said if anything happened to Daisy...'

'While she was with you,' Rachel finished for him. 'Yes, I remember.'

'There you go, then.'

'Well, I suppose accidents do happen,' said Rachel a little wearily. 'But you do realise she should have been wearing a life jacket, don't you?'

'Yeah, yeah.' Steve put both elbows on the table and ran his fingers through hair that was thinning at his temples. 'But Lauren had said, well, how pale Daisy's skin looked, and you don't get a tan wearing a life jacket all the time.'

Rachel shook her head. 'So, have you spoken to her today?'

'Daisy? Just to ask where you were.'

'You don't think she'd have appreciated you showing some concern?'

'Why?' Steve was offhand. 'She wants to go home, you know? I don't think Miami has lived up to her expectations.'

You mean you haven't, thought Rachel impatiently. 'And you and Lauren have other plans, right?' she suggested drily, and Steve gave her a quick look.

'What do you mean?'

'You're planning a trip to New York, aren't you?'

Steve's arms dropped onto the table. 'Who told you that?' He frowned. 'Was it Mendez?'

'Joe?' The word was out before she could prevent it, and she saw the familiarity hadn't gone unnoticed. But Steve had evidently decided not to push his luck, because all he said was, 'Yeah, Joe Mendez. I know he doesn't approve.'

'Doesn't he?' Knowing Joe as she was beginning to, that didn't surprise her.

'He takes too much upon himself,' muttered Steve petulantly. 'Spending time with Daisy. Meeting you at the airport. What was that all about?'

Rachel looked down at her coffee, hoping he wouldn't notice the sudden colour in her face. 'Well, you weren't planning on meeting me,' she pointed out quietly, and Steve made a sound of disgust.

'It would have been all the same if I was,' he countered aggressively. 'Since he offered Daisy a ride in his plane, he's done nothing but poke his nose into my affairs.'

'I'm sure that's not true.'

'Isn't it?' Steve shrugged. 'You don't know him like I do. I used to think he was my friend. Now I'm not so sure.'

Rachel lifted her head. 'Can I ask you something?'

Steve was wary. 'What?'

'Why did you lie about your age?'

'Oh, yeah.' Steve scowled at her. 'You couldn't wait to rat on me, could you? This is a young man's country, Rache. Why shouldn't I take off a few years? Plenty of women do.'

Rachel finished her coffee and put the cup aside. 'I'd better go,' she said. 'Daisy will be wondering where I am. Why don't you come with me?'

Steve made no attempt to move. 'She wants to go home, you know,' he said again. 'She wants to go back with you.'

Rachel shook her head. 'I don't think Dr Gonzales will allow that.'

'What do you mean?'

'It's too soon after the operation. She'll probably need a few more days' rest when she gets out of the clinic.'

'Well, I won't be here,' said Steve flatly. 'I've promised Lauren I'd take her to New York, and I can't let her down.'

'But you don't mind letting your daughter down?' Rachel suggested mildly. 'I think you need to go and see Daisy, Steve. Get your priorities in order.'

She excused herself to go to the bathroom, and when she came back Steve had gone.

CHAPTER ELEVEN

DAISY was alone when Rachel went back up to her room. Apart from asking if Rachel had seen her father, she seemed indifferent to the fact that he'd apparently left without saying goodbye. Rachel guessed that this was one of the reasons why she wanted to go home. Where Steve was concerned, only Lauren seemed to deserve his undivided attention.

Daisy fell asleep soon afterwards and Rachel took the opportunity to go back to her hotel and get changed. She could hardly go out for dinner in her tank top and shorts, and she was grateful now that she'd pushed the crocheted top and skirt she'd been wearing for her date with Paul Davis into the suitcase.

Then, before taking a shower, she rang Evelyn and Howard and told them what was going on.

Naturally, they were both disturbed to hear how serious Daisy's accident had been, and Evelyn said she'd give Steve a piece of her mind next time she was speaking to him. But Rachel knew that was unlikely. Since the rift between them had been breached, Steve's parents would be unlikely to do anything to create more hostility.

She rang off, promising to keep them informed of what was happening, and then took another shower. She even washed her hair again, aware that the heat and humidity had left a sticky film over her skin. Or was that being with Joe? she wondered, combing her hair back from her face and regarding her reflection with critical eyes. There was no doubt that when he touched her her temperature soared out of sight.

It was later than she'd expected when she got back to the hospital, and Daisy had already had her evening meal. She didn't appear to have missed her mother. When Rachel entered the room, she was engrossed in one of the films Joe had loaded onto the video iPod, but her eyes widened when she saw her mother had changed.

'That's new, isn't it?' she asked, and Rachel realised she'd bought it after Daisy had left for America.

'I had a date with Paul Davis,' she said offhandedly. 'I had to have something to wear.'

'It's nice.'

Daisy offered her approval before returning to the film, and Rachel spent the rest of the evening flicking through the magazines the nurse had brought her from the visitors' lounge. They didn't stop her nerves from jangling every time someone opened Daisy's door, but they helped keep her mind off seeing Joe again.

It was completely dark when she stepped outside later. But the heat hadn't dissipated. It wrapped itself around her like a damp blanket. Yet the scents of night-blooming blossoms seemed accentuated somehow, their fragrance giving the warm air a sensuous appeal.

Rachel had half expected Joe to be waiting for her in the foyer, but when the lift reached the ground floor only a female receptionist and two security guards were gathered about the desk. 'Have a pleasant evening, Ms Carlyle,' the receptionist called cheerfully, and Rachel was heartened by the fact that people were beginning to recognise her.

All the same, she wasn't happy standing out on the forecourt. At night, the clinic had a whole new ambience, and an awareness of how vulnerable she was to possible thieves or muggers couldn't help but cross her mind. After all, it was after nine o'clock. She couldn't remember when she'd last gone out so late at home. If ever.

When a low-slung dark vehicle swung into the grounds of the facility, Rachel drew back in alarm. The car was unfamiliar to her, and when it drove under the portico where she was standing she considered going back inside.

Then a window was lowered, and Joe said, 'Hey, Rachel!'

He was driving himself this evening, and he stopped the car beside her and thrust open his door. 'I'm late, I know,' he added, pulling a sheepish face. 'The traffic on the turnpike was murder.'

Rachel's tongue circled her lips. He had no idea how glad she was to see him. 'I haven't been waiting long,' she said quickly, and managed a slight smile when he looked down at her.

'You should have stayed inside,' he commented, his dark eyes taking an intense interest in her appearance. She was glad now she was wearing the new outfit. For the first time in his presence she didn't feel her age. 'A beautiful woman alone is always vulnerable.'

A beautiful woman! He'd said it again, and Rachel felt a shiver of anticipation slide down her spine. It didn't matter that she knew she wasn't beautiful. It was just so good to pretend she was.

'So…' Joe indicated the car behind him. 'Shall we get going?'

'Why not?' Rachel nodded, noticing how attractive he looked in lightweight cream trousers and a dark brown shirt. His collar was unfastened, and his folded-back sleeves displayed forearms liberally dusted with dark hair. There was a slim gold watch on his wrist, and a heavy gold ring occupied the smallest finger of his left hand. He was nothing like Steve, she thought. And wasn't she grateful for that?

The low sports-saloon had the distinctive smell of leather combined with what she recognised as an expensive men's cologne. And mingling with the rest was the singular scent of a heated male body.

The engine roared to life, and Joe swung the powerful vehicle out into the stream of traffic. Dozens of pairs of head-lights streamed towards them, illuminating palm trees and huge planters filled with flowering shrubs. Waxy anthuriums and scarlet proteas grew in careless profusion, reminding her of the semi-tropical climate, the heat of which had been briefly relieved by the fresh breeze blowing in her face.

'There's a tropical storm off Cuba,' Joe commented as she tucked her tumbled hair behind her ears. 'With a bit of luck, it won't come our way.' Then he smiled. 'How's Daisy tonight?'

Rachel thought how ironic it was that Joe seemed more concerned about her daughter than the girl's father. 'She's fine.' She paused. 'She really loves the video iPod. She's been watching one of the films you downloaded for her.'

'That would be fun for you.'

'Well, we did talk a little. Mostly about the fact that she wants to come home with me.'

'To England?'

'Hmm.' Rachel nodded. 'I've explained that Dr Gonzales might not agree. I've got an appointment to see him tomorrow morning.' She hesitated and then went on, 'I half wish she could. Steve has other plans, I think. He didn't expect this to happen.'

Joe's fingers tightened on the steering wheel. So Lauren had apparently got her way about the proposed trip to New York. He didn't know why he felt so angry about the way they were treating Daisy, but he did. She wasn't his daughter, but that didn't stop him from caring what happened to her.

'Why don't you stay on for a couple more weeks?' he found himself saying, almost without his own volition. 'I have a house on Biscayne Bay you could use. It would give Daisy time to recuperate.'

Rachel caught her breath. 'I couldn't do that.'

'Oh, right.' Joe frowned. 'You've got a deadline for your book. I'd forgotten about that.'

'The book's not a problem.' Rachel lifted her shoulders. 'I wouldn't be able to work if I was worrying about Daisy.'

'So what is the problem?' asked Joe quietly, bringing the powerful sports car to a halt outside what looked like a private dwelling. 'You don't want my help, is that it?' His eyes narrowed. 'What are you afraid of, Rachel? That I'll expect some personal compensation in lieu of rent?'

'No.' Rachel glanced anxiously towards the building they were parked outside, wondering if she'd been entirely wise to trust him after all. 'I—we, that is, Daisy and I—we can't stay in your house.' She shook her head. 'However innocent your offer is, it wouldn't be right.'

She thought Joe swore, but he thrust his door open without saying anything more and seconds later he was at her side of the vehicle, offering her his hand. His fingers were surprisingly cool considering the temperature, or perhaps it was the sweaty slipperiness of her own that made such a contrast.

Rachel's skirt slid along her thighs as she swung her feet to the pavement, and Joe felt another surge of frustration at the effect those slim bare legs had on his libido. For God's sake, what was wrong with him? She wasn't the kind of woman to get involved with. The word 'commitment' simply wasn't in his vocabulary.

Meanwhile Rachel was making an effort to smooth her tangled hair. Threading her fingers through it, she was intensely conscious of how her action exposed a provocative wedge of her midriff. Had Joe noticed? she speculated, her pulse quickening. Of course he had. She caught her breath. Was he wondering how far she was prepared to go?

The appearance of a young man wearing a black waistcoat over a crisp white shirt and pin-striped trousers brought a welcome breath of sanity to the situation. 'Evenin', Mr

Mendez,' he greeted Joe familiarly. 'Evenin', ma'am; welcome to the *Sea House*. And how are y'all this evening? Hopin' that tropical storm gives us a wide berth, I'll bet?'

'You got it.' Joe forced a smile and handed over his car keys. Then Rachel felt his hand in the small of her back. 'Come on.' He ushered her up the steps into a lamplit foyer. 'The food here is excellent. I always come at least once when I'm in Miami.'

The *maître d'* met them in the foyer; a short, dark-skinned man of Latino ancestry, he greeted Joe like a long-lost brother. 'Joe, my man,' he said, shaking Joe's hand warmly. 'I heard you were in the city and I was wondering if you were going to pay us a visit this time around.'

'Would I miss tasting your seared sea bass?' asked Joe good-naturedly, his hand slipping naturally about Rachel's waist. 'Meet Henri Libre, Rachel. He's another South American exile who's made a name for himself in Miami and New York.'

'How do you do?'

Rachel allowed the little man to take her hand, supremely conscious when Joe's fingers moved against her skin. If his intention was to ensure she was aware of him, he was wasting his time. She'd been aware of no one else since he'd arrived at the clinic.

The restaurant was through opaque glass doors, and it was instantly cooler once the doors closed behind them. Henri offered them a drink at the adjoining bar, and Joe asked her if she'd like a cocktail. 'You must try Antonio's margaritas,' he said, nodding to the barman. 'He makes the best cocktails in the city.'

Rachel was helped onto a stool at the bar, and presently a broad-rimmed glass was set in front of her. 'Try it,' Joe said, watching her. 'I've told Antonio to hold the salt.'

The tequila caught the back of Rachel's throat, and for a moment she felt as if she couldn't get her breath. Then the alcohol found its way to her stomach and she took a steadying gulp of air. The last thing she needed was to get tipsy, she thought. Being with Joe was intoxicating enough as it was.

Leaving her glass on the bar, she half turned to survey the room behind her. From what she could see, the restaurant was small and intimate, lamplit booths and carefully arranged trellises of greenery providing both privacy and anonymity for the guests. Which was probably why Joe liked it, she reflected a little cynically. A man of his wealth and power was bound to attract attention wherever he went. Yet, despite his obvious attraction for women, he didn't strike her as the kind of man who would court notoriety.

'Don't you like it?'

Joe, who she noticed had accepted only a soft drink, drew her attention, and she swung round again, bumping her knees against his. 'Oh, sorry,' she said as he parted his legs to accommodate her. But instead of allowing her to move back to the bar, he imprisoned her knees between both of his.

'My pleasure,' he said. 'So, tell me, do you like the margarita?'

Rachel glanced at the drink. 'It's very nice,' she said breathily. Then, in an effort to distract herself, 'You're only drinking tonic.'

'I need to keep my head around you,' said Joe huskily. His eyes darkened as they rested on her mouth. A tiny drop of liquid rested on her lower lip, and before he could stop himself he'd leant forward and captured it with his tongue. 'Have you any idea how good you taste?'

Rachel swallowed. 'I don't think you should make fun of me,' she protested, and Joe stifled a rueful laugh.

'Oh, baby,' he said. 'I'm not making fun of you.' He hesitated, and then continued roughly, 'Myself, maybe. I'm the one who's drowning here.'

Rachel shook her head. 'You don't have to flatter me.'

'For God's sake!' Joe swore then. 'I'm not flattering you, damn it.' His hands dug into her knees for a moment and then he released her. 'Hell, that ex-husband of yours did some number on you, didn't he?'

'I don't know what you mean.' Rachel reached for the margarita again, needing the punch of the alcohol to steady her nerves.

'Sure you do,' said Joe, his expression sardonic. 'But okay, we'll play it your way. For the time being, at least.'

Thankfully, Henri returned to offer them menus, and then later to ask what they'd like for dinner, and for the next few minutes Rachel was able to pretend she wasn't out of her depth. But she had to admit that Joe's analogy had been apt—though she was the one who was drowning, not him.

Eventually, they were shown to a table by the windows. The lamplight was reflected in the glass and Rachel realised why the restaurant was called the *Sea House*. Their booth overlooked a rocky promontory, and discreetly placed lights illuminated the water below. There was no moon, but the restless waves lapping against the shoreline were distinctly audible.

She ate scallops with tempura vegetables, and an escalope of seared sea bass with a delicate truffle sauce. The food, as Joe had told her, was delicious, and despite her nerves Rachel found herself enjoying it.

Joe chose the wine, and if she'd reserved judgment about the margarita she had no such doubts about the smooth Chablis. It slid effortlessly down her throat, and she hardly noticed that the waiter refilled her glass several times throughout the meal. It was all wonderful, and unbelievably relaxed, and she was sorry when the time came for them to leave.

'I've had such a good time,' she said, regarding Joe with shining eyes. 'I don't know what else to say.'

'You could say you'll accept my offer of the house on Biscayne Bay,' Joe murmured, capturing her hand that was lying beside her plate. His thumb probed the sensitive veins on the inner side of her wrist before sliding down to caress her palm. 'I really wish you would.'

Rachel sucked in a breath. 'And what would you do?'

'Me?' Joe lifted her hand and rubbed his lips against her knuckles. 'You don't think I'm suggesting we should share the place, do you?'

Rachel hesitated, her stomach fluttering nervously. 'You—you're not?'

'No.' Joe regarded her over her quivering fingers. 'I told you, I have a condo on Miami Beach. The house on Biscayne Bay has been in my family for years. My sister used to live there before she moved to Los Angeles. I never have.'

'Oh!' Rachel was nonplussed.

'Does it make a difference?'

It shouldn't have, really, but she couldn't deny it did. If Daisy had to stay in the United States for a while, it would be so much better for her than living at the *Park Plaza* hotel.

'Maybe,' she said at last, withdrawing her hand as Joe got to his feet. 'Can I think about it?'

Joe shrugged, but Henri Libre was at his elbow, and he didn't say anything more until they were outside the building. Then, as the valet went to get his car, he bent his lips to her ear. 'Why don't I show you the place? It might help you make up your mind.'

A particularly strong breeze caused Rachel to sway a little, and she wasn't sure if it was the wind or the amount of wine she'd consumed that made her feel so unsteady suddenly. But when Joe stepped closer, and slipped a protective arm around her waist, she knew she didn't want the evening to end.

'Yes,' she said, barely audibly, and wondered exactly what she was agreeing to.

The valet reappeared with Joe's car, and after brief farewells they were on their way. It was quite late; after midnight,

Rachel guessed—but there was still plenty of traffic on the main highway.

She leaned her head back against the soft leather squabs and closed her eyes for a moment. It had been a wonderful evening, she thought, guiltily aware that she'd only thought of her daughter very fleetingly. But it was so long since she'd allowed herself any real indulgence whatsoever.

An awareness that the sound of the traffic was fading caused her to open her eyes again, and they widened in dismay when she realised they were heading in the wrong direction. She was sure they'd driven south from Palm Cove, and they were still driving south, with the lights of the city behind them.

She was about to voice her concerns when Joe took the off-ramp into a residential suburb. Here the streets were quieter, even deserted at times. Houses sheltered behind iron gates and high stone walls that were overhung with vines and bougainvillea. Some of the roads were lined with trees, palms and live oaks, the scents of night-blooming stocks mingling with the tang of the sea. Their exotic fragrance invaded the car, a heady mix of salt and sweetness.

'Where are we?' she exclaimed, not exactly worried, but not exactly relaxed either. She was sure this wasn't the way back to her hotel.

'We're in Coral Gables,' replied Joe casually as they negotiated a cross street where the signs were predominantly Spanish. 'It's an attractive neighbourhood. In actual fact, it considers itself a separate city within the Greater Miami area.'

Rachel licked her suddenly dry lips. 'And we're here because…?' Though she suspected she already knew.

'You said you'd let me show you the house we were discussing earlier,' said Joe, glancing her way. 'Don't worry. It's not much farther.'

Rachel let out a nervous breath as they turned onto a yet narrower road. She glimpsed a sign that read *Viejo Avenida*, which she thought meant Old Avenue. But the headlights were already illuminating wooden gates ahead, bright with scarlet hibiscus.

'This is it,' said Joe, and as if by magic the gates opened to allow them through. 'Don't be put off by all this vegetation. If it bothers you, I'll have Ramon cut it back.'

'Oh, no.'

The involuntary denial was out before she could prevent it. But although she couldn't yet see much of the house, Rachel thought the gardens were a delight. The headlights swept over an old banyan tree guarding what appeared to be a stone fountain; the fountain gleamed with lichen, a stone angel pouring water from a stone urn.

The drive was enclosed by kudzu and oleander, and a covered porch was cloaked with flowering vines. Rachel saw this before Joe doused his headlights, and in the shadows she saw him looking at her now.

'Would you care to see inside?'

CHAPTER TWELVE

How could she refuse?

Besides, sitting here in the darkness, she felt far more aware of him than she would be in the house. 'If you like,' she said, trying to sound casual. She pushed open the door and got out into the almost total blackness. The air seemed marginally cooler here.

How far away was the sea?

She heard the gates close behind them, and guessed Joe had used whatever instrument had opened them on their arrival to complete the task. Evidently her hope that Ramon, whoever he was, had opened them at their approach was wishful thinking. There were no lights that she could see anywhere. Joe even produced a flashlight to guide them to the front door.

He handed the torch to her as he found the key, and the door swung inward. Half expecting a draught of musty air—usual when a house had been unoccupied for a while—Rachel was pleasantly surprised when the air inside seemed relatively fresh. Scented, even, she thought, smelling verbena. Someone looked after the place. As Joe Mendoza was the owner, what else could she have expected?

Nevertheless, it was quite a relief when Joe found the switch and the interior was suddenly illuminated. She turned off the flashlight as Joe closed the door behind them, her breath catching in her throat at the beauty of her surroundings.

The house was old. That was obvious. Probably built in the twenties, she suspected, and extravagantly designed accordingly. An Italian-marble tiled foyer gave access to a handful of rooms, all elegantly furnished from what Rachel could see. Lots of rich wood and fine leather; Tiffany lamps gleaming in the reflected light from the hall.

The walls of the hall were panelled in pale oak, and boasted a gallery of art-nouveau paintings that she guessed were worth a small fortune. A staircase that folded back on itself climbed the far wall, a stained-glass window at the first landing highlighted by a Venetian glass chandelier.

'Welcome to *Bahia Mar*,' said Joe lightly. 'As you've probably guessed, the house backs onto the water.'

Rachel took a breath. 'I thought I could smell the sea.'

'Yeah. Well, one of the waterways that runs into the bay,' agreed Joe, glancing about him. 'Let's go into the living room. I'll switch on the outside lights for you to see the garden.'

Beyond French doors, a paved terrace looked inviting. Chairs and loungers were set around a table, whose canvas awning was securely tied against the wind. Rachel noticed how the bushes surrounding the terrace were bending in the current of air that blew off the water. Joe slid the door back only wide enough for them to step outside.

Despite the wind, the air was still hot and humid, the whirring of the night insects strong in Rachel's ears as she stared out beyond the reassuring circle of light. She could hear the sucking sound of the water, but it was too dark to see much more. Yet all around her the garden seemed alive with an odd kind of excitement, an excitement that couldn't help but quicken her awareness of the man beside her.

'I keep a boat here sometimes,' Joe offered as she went to grip the wooden rail that separated the terrace from a veritable jungle of tropical vegetation. Thick vines bent in the wind, scattering raindrops in all directions. 'Be careful,' he warned as she moved to where a flight of steps disappeared into the darkness. 'It rained earlier, and they're probably slippery as hell.'

Rachel decided to take his advice and stay where she was. Much as she would have liked to go farther, she would prefer to do so in daylight when she could see where she was putting her feet. Not all visitors to the garden would be friendly, she reflected. She could imagine how she'd feel if she stepped on a snake or a huge spider.

'The dock is at the other end of the garden,' said Joe, touching her elbow. 'I'd show you, but we'd both get soaked to the skin.'

Which was as good an excuse as any to take their clothes off, he thought, even if getting naked with Rachel might not be such a good idea. He'd promised her dinner; that had been all. And he was trying to keep his word.

Nevertheless, showing her the house at night when he'd known Ramon and his wife, who looked after the place for him, had retired to their quarters in the grounds wasn't the wisest idea he'd ever had. Not when Rachel was looking so delectable, her silky hair tumbled by the wind.

He closed and locked the French doors after they'd returned to the house, and then followed Rachel back into the entrance hall. He watched as she looked about her, studying her surroundings, touching the delicate petals of an orchid, gliding her fingers over the polished surface of a chest his father had brought back from Venezuela.

'Well,' he said, resisting the urge to touch her again. 'What do you think?'

'About the house?' Rachel shrugged, and when she did so the neckline of her top slipped seductively off one shoulder. 'It's beautiful,' she answered, seemingly unaware of what had happened. 'More beautiful than I could ever have imagined.'

'So?' Joe's enquiry was unnaturally tight.

Rachel hesitated. Then she looked up at him, her green eyes wide and appealing. 'Do you think I could see upstairs?' she asked, and Joe felt an unfamiliar tension in his gut.

'Upstairs?' He sucked in a breath.

'Unless we'd be disturbing anyone,' she said. 'You mentioned—Ramon, was it?'

'Ramon and Maria—his wife—look after the place,' Joe told her swiftly. 'They have their own quarters separate from the house.'

'So it's all right if I look upstairs?'

Joe regarded her tensely. 'If that's what you want.'

'It is.' Rachel was amazed at her own temerity. 'How many bedrooms are there?'

She'd started up the marble staircase as she spoke, slim, bare legs revealing a shapely calf to his helpless eyes. Joe knew he had to follow her. She'd expect it. But damn it, what was going on here? He had the uneasy feeling that he'd lost control of the situation.

Rachel stopped, looking down at him enquiringly, and he realised she was waiting for his reply. 'Um, six,' he said, forcing his brain to think of something other than the memory of how her mouth had felt when he'd kissed her. 'You—you and Daisy could choose any two you liked.'

'Hmm.'

Rachel nodded before continuing on to the top of the second flight. Then, her hand resting on the sculpted balustrade, she waited for him to join her. The landing stretched away in a semi-circle, wrought-iron spindles shadowy in the muted light from below.

Joe located the switch that illuminated a row of alcoves along a carpeted hallway that led away from the landing and, going ahead, he threw open the door into what used to be the master suite. Stepping back, he allowed her to precede him into the room.

A lamp beside the four-poster bed provided enough illumination for her to admire the traditional-style furniture. Oak chests of drawers, a tall armoire, tapestry-covered armchairs with matching footstools. Most of the floor was concealed beneath an enormous hand-woven carpet, the dark-wood boards surrounding it polished to a rich shine. Filmy sheers hung at long windows, pale against the night outside.

Rachel had expected to be impressed, and she was. The house—its appointments—were all she had imagined and more. Somehow, because of Joe's background in computers, she'd been prepared for something slick and modern. But *Bahia Mar* had all the beauty of a bygone age.

She could never stay here, she thought regretfully. As much as she admired the place, she simply couldn't see herself going to bed in a room like this. Her whole wardrobe would probably fit in the armoire, let alone the adjoining dressing room. And she hadn't seen the bathroom yet. It would probably be a homage to sensual indulgence too.

She wondered suddenly if Joe brought all his women here. How many women had shared the luxury of that four-poster bed? He said he didn't live here, but that didn't mean he hadn't stayed here. It was the ideal hideaway for the man who liked his privacy.

Joe was still standing by the door, watching her, and Rachel wondered what he was thinking. Evidently her fear—or was that anticipation?—that he'd brought her here to seduce her had been totally unfounded. She'd really thought, earlier that evening, that he'd wanted more than the breathtaking kiss they'd shared at the bar. And while the sane and sensible part of her brain applauded his restraint—if that was what it was— the excitement she'd felt in the garden was in her blood.

Apart from that ghastly evening at Julie Corbett's, she'd been celibate for the past eight—or was that nine?—years.

She and Steve had separated long before he'd moved out of the house. Why shouldn't she take a chance for once? Why shouldn't she have at least one night to remember?

It took some courage, but she crossed to the four-poster and flopped down on one side of the bed. The bed might be old, but the mattress was new and bouncy, the cream silk coverlet cool beneath her bare thighs.

Joe hadn't moved, his dark face unreadable in the shadowy light. Had he stiffened, or was that just her imagination? He was probably thinking she was crazy, she reflected. She hadn't exactly encouraged him to think that she wanted more.

She felt so hot, an aching longing stirring deep in her belly. Her whole body felt tingly and alive with needs she'd almost forgotten. And she certainly couldn't remember an occasion when Steve had made her feel that, if he hadn't touched her, she'd have died of frustration.

Turning, she raised one knee to the coverlet, aware that as she did so almost the whole length of her other leg was exposed. Then, sliding her hand over the smooth silk, she raised her eyes to his taut face. 'Do you mind if I try it?'

Try what? wondered Joe grimly, a pulse throbbing at his jawline. Did she realise what her childish display was doing to him? Did she know how amazingly sexy she was? Probably not, he decided. But that didn't change how he felt.

'Do you need my permission?' he asked now, an edge to his tone. 'You seem to be enjoying yourself.'

'I am.' Rachel's skirt rucked high above her knees as she clambered onto the pile of pillows Maria had arranged below the headboard, and Joe caught a glimpse of white lace before she subsided onto her back. She dug her heels into the coverlet and raised her arms high above her head. 'Mmm, it's so comfortable.' She turned her head towards him. 'But I'm sure you know that.'

Joe's face was tense. 'What's that supposed to mean?'

'Oh…' Rachel considered her words before replying. 'I'm sure you've slept in this bed before.'

Joe shook his head. 'No.'

'No?' She rolled onto her side to face him. 'So which room do you usually use?'

'Believe it or not, but I've never stayed here,' he said harshly. 'What do you think it is? Some kind of *love nest*?'

Suddenly Rachel felt very embarrassed—and very cheap. She sat up abruptly. 'I'm sorry,' she said. 'You must think I'm very rude and very ungrateful.' She swung her legs towards the side of the bed. 'Perhaps we ought to go now. It was good of you to show me the house, but I'm afraid I'm going to have to refuse your offer.'

Joe blew out a breath. He'd upset her now and that hadn't been his intention. He had to remember she wasn't like the women he was used to associating with. And while that ought to be enough to cool his ardour, somehow it didn't.

Rachel dropped her feet to the floor and bent, searching for the heels she'd discarded earlier. When a pair of black suede loafers moved into her line of vision, she looked up in astonishment, her gaze moving over powerful legs, a flat stomach and a broad chest to a lean, disturbing face. She also registered the prominent bulge at the junction of his thighs, but her eyes skittered away from its obvious significance.

'What offer would that be?' Joe asked, squatting down in front of her so that their eyes were almost on a level. 'I thought for a moment you had something to offer me.'

Rachel shook her head. 'I was being silly,' she said hurriedly. She dragged her eyes away and glanced down at her feet. 'Where on earth did I leave my shoes?'

Joe was silent for a moment and then he leant towards her, supporting himself with a hand at either side of her. 'Forget your shoes,' he said huskily, bestowing a feather-light kiss on the pulse that beat so erratically below her ear. 'I was thinking of taking your clothes off, not putting them on.'

Rachel's mouth opened and she stared at him disbelievingly. 'You don't have to say that,' she protested quickly. 'I mean, you really don't.'

Joe uttered a low laugh. 'Hey, don't bail on me now, sweetheart. There's only so much provocation a man can take.'

Rachel drew back onto her elbows, her heart racing. 'I— I didn't mean to provoke you,' she said, although she had. But she was no *femme fatale,* and she suspected he was just being kind.

'Well, you did,' Joe countered, his voice thickening. 'But don't worry about it.' He put his hands on her knees, and pushed himself to his feet. Then, straddling her legs, he moved until his own knees nudged the side of the bed. 'As a matter of fact, you've been provoking me all evening.'

'Joe…'

'Rachel,' he said gently, resting one knee on the mattress beside her. His thumb brushed her jawline as he tilted her face towards him. 'You don't think you're the only one who has feelings, do you?'

Oh, God!

When he bent and captured her mouth with his, Rachel's mind spiralled. He pressed her back against the pillows, supporting himself on his hands. The scent of his skin teased her senses, and her body felt both weak and yet incredibly strong.

Her lips parted, and Joe's tongue pushed urgently into her mouth. He kissed her with a hunger that amazed him. It was becoming harder and harder to control the urge to rub his aching erection against her, but he knew if he allowed that to happen she'd know instantly how aroused he was.

She lifted a hand to his cheek, soft fingers stroking the roughness at his jawline, probing the sensitive hollow of his ear. Her hand slipped to the nape of his neck, pulling him closer, and despite all his good intentions Joe couldn't keep that small distance between them.

And touching her meant giving in to the emotions that were driving him on. The lissom feel of her body beneath his was all he'd imagined and more. He had to admit, if only to himself, that he'd never wanted a woman as he wanted Rachel at that moment. Feeling her breasts crushed beneath his chest, the intimacy of his leg wedged between her thighs, was driving him crazy.

His mouth trailed from her lips to her throat, to the scented hollow of her cleavage just visible above the neckline of her crocheted top. He let his hand slide beneath the top, his palm spreading against the firm, warm flesh of her midriff. Her skin was like silk, but he'd known that. It wasn't as if he'd never touched her before.

His mouth found hers again and this time her tongue came to mate with his. The kiss deepened, hardened, and between his legs the erection he'd been trying to ignore for the past hour demanded satisfaction. It didn't help at all when she arched up against him and her hip brushed the almost painful swelling in his trousers. It only added to his frustration, to the needs he could no longer do without.

He groaned and Rachel's eyes flickered open. 'Is something wrong?' she asked, unaware of the sensual invitation in her voice.

'Yeah.' Joe gritted his teeth. 'I want you.' He threaded his fingers through the hair above her ear and managed a rueful smile. 'But I guess this is the point where I offer to take you home.'

Rachel looked up at him with eyes that shredded his good intentions. 'I don't think that's what you really want, do you?'

'What I really want?' Joe closed his eyes for a moment, struggling with his conscience. 'What I really want is to have you naked beneath me. To know you want me as much as I want you.'

Rachel took a deep breath. 'Well, I do,' she confessed honestly. 'But, well, it's been a long time since I allowed a man into my life.'

'Yeah.' Joe bent and allowed his tongue to probe her mouth before adding softly, 'I guessed. Despite the sexy seduction.'

Rachel's cheeks were flushed with pleasure. 'Am I sexy?'

'You better believe it.' Joe spoke a little thickly. 'And I'm flattered that you trust me. It means a lot.'

Rachel hesitated. 'Do you think I'm desperate for affection?' she asked uneasily, and Joe stifled his laugh against her neck.

'Hey, I'm the one who's desperate,' he said, his voice roughening as he unbuttoned her bodice. His eyes darkened when he saw her breasts fairly spilling from the lacy bra she was wearing. 'But we'll talk about that later. Right now, I've got something else in mind.'

CHAPTER THIRTEEN

HER bra followed her top onto the floor, and Joe made a sound of satisfaction as he bent to take a swollen nipple into his mouth. He nibbled at the hardened tip, his teeth giving more pleasure than pain, his tongue caressing the rosy areola until Rachel was shifting restlessly beneath him.

He skimmed his hand over her ribcage, his fingers lingering over her navel. A sexy little moan drove him onwards, and when he baulked at the waistline of her skirt she shifted to allow him to slide the offending garment over her hips.

'Beautiful,' he said, bending to bestow a trail of kisses across her stomach. Her panties were surprisingly flimsy and he tugged gently at the elastic, sending a quiver of anticipation into her thighs.

Rachel's mouth seemed dry of all moisture. Her breathing was shallow, her breasts rising and falling with increasing urgency as he parted her legs. Then, with exquisite delicacy, he drew her panties down her legs and replaced their small amount of protection with his hand.

She was wet, he discovered as the sensual smell of her arousal rose unmistakeably to his nose, and he groaned a little as he lowered his head to taste her essence. 'Sweet,' he muttered huskily as she twisted breathlessly beneath him. 'I knew you'd taste as good as you look.'

'Please…'

Rachel wasn't used to this sensual assault on her senses. Her hands groped for his head, wanting him to go on doing what he was doing, and at the same time wanting so much more. Heavens, she was virtually naked, and he was still wearing his clothes.

'Relax,' he said, lifting his head, his eyes dark with unguarded emotion. Then, ripping open the buttons of his shirt, he sent it to join her clothes on the floor. She caught her breath at the sight of his chest, at the dark tattoo of an exotic orchid twisting over his shoulder. And thought that only a man as comfortable with his masculinity as Joe would allow a flower, however intriguing, to be etched on his skin.

His shoulders were broad, his stomach flat and ribbed with muscle, and an arrowing of dark hair found its way from his chest to disappear below the waistband of his trousers. His zip bulged with the thrust of his erection and, with a daring she hadn't known she possessed, she let her nails stroke provocatively over the taut metal.

Joe groaned again, reaching for his buckle and pulling it free. Seconds later, he'd kicked off his trousers, and his shaft sprang sensuously into her waiting hands.

'Be gentle with me,' he muttered half-humorously as she let her fingers slide over his length, amazed that he was still in control. But he sucked in a breath when her thumb found the sensitive tip, and she wriggled down to take a bead of moisture into her mouth.

Joe moved then, bearing her back against the cushions again, and taking her mouth in another devastating kiss. 'God, Rachel,' he muttered, releasing her mouth at last to bury his face in the scented hollow of her shoulder. 'I want you so much. And I don't think I can wait any longer.'

'Then take me,' she said tremulously, lifting his head to cradle it between her hands. 'I want you too, in case you hadn't noticed.'

He parted her legs then, kneeling between them and nudging the swollen nub of her womanhood with his aching shaft. But the sight of her delectable body—open and ready for him—was too tempting to ignore, and with a feeling of satisfaction he pushed into her waiting sheath.

She was so tight that he could hardly believe she'd had a baby. And despite her vain boast of experience, it was obvious it had been a long time since any man had made love to her. Which pleased him greatly, he acknowledged, aware of his own selfishness at the thought. He wanted her not to be experienced, he realised. He wanted this to be a new intimacy. And judging by the way she was responding to him, he was going to get his wish.

But then the urgency of his own needs took over. Taking her mouth again, he eased into her completely, feeling her muscles contract around him with supreme pleasure. She was tight, but she fitted him perfectly. Their bodies could have been made for one another, and when he pulled back and pushed into her again, the sound they made was like music to his ears.

Quickening the pace, he felt her muscles tighten. She was so hot, so responsive, and he knew she was close to climax when her nails dug painfully into his neck.

'Take it easy, baby,' he said, despite the fact that his own control was slipping. But when she lifted her legs and wound them about his hips there was no holding back.

The developing spasms of her orgasm were gripping him, and he didn't attempt to hold back his own release. The sensation that overtook him proved he was experiencing something he'd never experienced before. He shuddered uncontrollably for what seemed like hours, but was probably only for a few minutes, his hips pumping every drop of moisture from his body.

Belatedly, he acknowledged that he should have drawn back before he climaxed. But with her arms around his neck and her ankles digging into his buttocks, he doubted he'd have had the strength. Besides, he'd never had such a feeling of completeness. He felt drained, shattered, barely able to drag himself away from her before slumping heavily onto the bed beside her.

He thought he must have slept for a while. When he opened his eyes again, it was still dark outside, but he was alone. The space where Rachel had been lying was empty. And when he smoothed his hand over the coverlet he found it was already cold.

Pushing himself up onto his elbows, he stared broodingly around the room. Where the hell was she? There was no sound from the bathroom, so he was fairly sure she wasn't in there. Damn, where had she got to? Surely she hadn't done something stupid like leave the house?

Joe didn't feel like getting up. His body was still in that pleasant state of inertia that follows really good sex, and all he really wanted to do was make love with Rachel all over again. The way he felt right now, he'd have been happy to spend the rest of the night making love with her. But he sensed that wasn't going to happen. Not when he didn't know where the hell she was.

He scowled, aware that he'd never been in this situation before. He'd always been the one to call the shots in a relationship. And it hadn't escaped his attention that he was using the words 'making love' far too frequently.

His scowl deepened, and kicking the covers aside, he got up from the bed. His body ached a little as he bent to grab his trousers from the floor, and that only added to his frustration. This was not supposed to happen. What had happened to his no-strings policy, for heaven's sake?

Leaving the button at his waist unfastened—this was so not over, he told himself—he shouldered into his shirt and caught a glimpse of himself in the long cheval-mirror across the room. He looked grim, he thought. And petulant. Not a good look for someone hoping to persuade another person that they were making a big mistake.

Breathing deeply, he took a moment to calm himself. Then, leaving the bedroom, he made his way to the top of the stairs. What the hell time was it anyway? he wondered, trying to focus on the face of his watch. It looked like a quarter to four. He blinked. Was it possible? Of course it was. Rachel could be miles away by now.

There was no sound from downstairs either, and he made no attempt to muffle his footsteps as he descended to the hall below. No lights, he noted. Well, if she was still here, she was certainly keeping a low profile.

His stomach clenched. He didn't want to accept that he was worried about her, but he was. Damn it, did she blame him for what had happened? Or was she feeling guilty because, for the first time in goodness knew how long, she'd taken some time for herself? Time that didn't include Daisy.

Daisy!

He scowled again. He liked the kid; of course he did. But it bugged him that she was appropriating so much of Rachel's time when her father had eschewed all responsibility for his daughter. Still, without Steve he'd never have met Rachel, and whatever beef he had with Carlyle, that was a situation he didn't care to contemplate right now.

With an increasing sense of desperation, he searched all the ground-floor rooms, even going into the kitchen on the off chance that she might have decided to get herself a drink. But then the memory of that cold place beside him intruded, and he realised that she could have made herself a dozen drinks in the time it had taken for the bed to cool.

He went back into the living room, not switching on the lamps this time, and made his way by the light streaming in from the hall to the bar. Pouring himself a generous shot of bourbon, he raised the glass to his lips. But before he could take a drink something moving on the patio outside attracted his attention.

He slammed the glass back down onto the counter, uncaring that he spilled some of the whisky in the process, and moved to the sliding-glass doors. Whatever it was he'd seen seemed to have disappeared, and with the wind tossing leaves and flower petals across the paved area, it was easy to explain what had distracted him.

But then, as he turned away, he saw a flutter of turquoise cotton flapping against one of the loungers. He stared for a moment, hardly daring to believe his eyes, and then realised that it was indeed Rachel, sitting outside, apparently unaware, or uncaring, that she'd practically scared him out of his mind.

He didn't think before opening the door. The slider slammed back against its housing and Rachel's wide, startled gaze turned in his direction. 'Oh,' she said ineffectually. 'You're awake.'

'Yes, I'm awake.' It was an effort to keep the anger out of his voice, and he doubted he had. 'What the hell are you doing, sitting out here? Don't you know I've spent the last half hour looking for you?'

'I—no.' Rachel got to her feet a little unsteadily, but Joe refused to feel any sympathy for her. She'd scared the hell out of him! 'I just needed some air.'

'Air?' Joe was scathing. 'You call this air?'

'Well, the wind is refreshing,' she said defensively. Then, as if recovering a little of her spirit, 'I didn't know I had to report all my movements to you.'

Joe closed his eyes for a moment. Then, raking his nails over his scalp, he said roughly, 'You don't, of course. I'm sorry. I was—worried, that's all.'

He saw her stiffen. 'You don't have to worry about me. I'm used to taking care of myself.'

'Yeah, yeah.' Joe realised he was going about this in entirely the wrong way. 'But I was worried. I thought— Well, never mind what I thought.' He glanced behind him. 'Let's go back inside.'

Rachel hesitated, but after a moment she moved towards the house. She had to pass Joe as she did so, but when he put out a reassuring hand to grip her upper arm she flinched away from his touch. With an air of injured dignity, she went past him, not stopping until she was standing in the middle of the entrance hall.

Joe slammed the glass door closed and then paused in the living-room doorway, raising one hand to support himself on the lintel above his head. He was aware that his action caused his zip to open a little wider, but he didn't try to stop it. If she could see what being with her was doing to him, then so be it. Maybe it would achieve what his attempt at conciliation had not.

However, when she said nothing, he had to try again. 'Look,' he said, 'Why don't we take this upstairs? It'll be morning soon. Then I'll take you back to your hotel.'

Rachel held up her head. 'I'd like to go now, please. I would have called a cab, but I didn't know the number.' She bit her lip as another thought occurred to her. 'I'm assuming they don't lock the doors after midnight or anything like that?'

'Hardly.' Joe knew a cynical desire to laugh. The idea of a hotel like the *Park Plaza* locking its doors before half its patrons were in residence was too ludicrous to call. He sucked in a breath. 'Don't go,' he said huskily. 'I realise I've upset you, but that's just the way I am. This evening has meant a lot to me, damn it. Can't we go back to where we were before you decided to take a walk on the wild side?'

'I didn't—' began Rachel, and then realised he didn't mean that in reality. 'And I'm sorry if I worried you. I didn't consider how you might react when you found I wasn't with you.'

Joe managed a rueful smile. 'I guess not,' he agreed,

dropping his arm and taking a step towards her. 'So, why don't we begin again?' His eyes darkened. 'Do you have any idea how sexy you look without any make-up?' He shook his head. 'Not many women can say that.'

'And you've known quite a few,' murmured Rachel, retreating a step so the distance between them remained the same.

Joe's smile disappeared. 'That has nothing to do with us,' he said. 'For God's sake, Rachel, you're not going to bring my past into this, are you?'

'Why not?' Rachel had had plenty of time to think while she'd sat out on the patio, and although she'd discovered that she didn't regret what had happened, she'd decided it was never going to happen again. It was too dangerous. She wasn't cut out for this kind of relationship, and while she'd been flattered that he'd wanted her, she had the distinct feeling that the only person likely to get hurt in this situation was herself.

And wasn't that a joke?

'Rachel…'

Joe was tired and frustrated, and her attitude baffled him. He should have had that drink while he'd had the chance, he thought. It might have helped him to make sense of what was going on.

'What was it Steve said?' Rachel continued. She frowned. 'Oh, yes: that this is a young man's country. Well, I guess that applies to women as well.'

Joe's brows drew together. 'You've been talking to Steve?'

'Yes.' Rachel nodded. 'He came to the hospital this afternoon.'

Joe felt a twinge of something he refused to recognise as jealousy. 'Was Lauren with him?'

'No.'

'And you didn't think to tell me?'

Rachel's eyes widened. 'Why should I tell you?'

'Oh, I don't know.' Joe scowled. 'Maybe because I thought my opinion mattered to you.'

Rachel sighed. 'It does.' She took a deep breath. 'He didn't stay long.'

Joe hesitated. 'And how did you feel? Seeing him again after—what's it been?—a year?'

'Slightly more than that.' Rachel shrugged. 'It was okay. I felt sorry for him, actually.'

'*Sorry* for him?' Joe couldn't keep the frustration out of his voice now. 'What are you saying? That you still care about the guy? That even after the way he's behaved—'

'No, no.' Rachel interrupted him. 'It's been a long time since I cared about Steve Carlyle.'

'So that's not what all this is about?'

'Steve?' Rachel didn't pretend not to understand. 'No!'

Joe could feel his pulse quickening, anger causing the blood to rush headlong through his veins. 'Then what is happening here?' he demanded. 'I thought you wanted this just as much as I did. You certainly gave me that impression. So what did I do wrong?'

Rachel hardly knew how to answer him. 'I— You didn't do anything wrong,' she murmured unhappily. 'It's just, well, it was good while it lasted, but it's over now—'

'Like hell!'

'It is.' It took an effort, but she raised her eyes to his face. 'I like you, Joe. I like you a lot. And I know I owe you a lot, too. Daisy and I both do.'

'You don't owe me.' Joe was incensed, as much with his own unfamiliar emotions as by what Rachel was saying. 'I just don't understand what's going on.'

Rachel took a step backward. 'I'm sorry,' she said. 'Maybe I'm not explaining myself very well.'

'You're not!'

'I just don't think we should see one another again.'

'Are you crazy?' Joe swore then, and she took another step back.

'I'm sorry,' she said again. 'I know I probably seem very old-fashioned, but that's what comes of living a fairly conservative life. And whatever impression I've given you, I don't do this sort of thing.'

'What sort of thing?'

'Sleep with men I hardly know,' she replied quickly. 'You might not believe this after—well, after Steve—but I still believe in marriage; in commitment. For Daisy's sake, I have to think of the future. Our future. And we both know this was not what being with you was all about.'

Joe stared at her. And then said something he never thought he'd hear coming from his mouth. 'How do you know that?'

'Oh, please.' Rachel heaved a sigh. 'Don't pretend. When you invited me out, you admitted you'd have no trouble finding another date.'

'Maybe I was bragging.' Joe's jaw compressed.

'I don't think so.'

'So I've had girlfriends. What's so unusual about that? You went out with some guy yourself back in England.'

Rachel closed her eyes for a moment. 'Paul Davis is just a friend. I told you that.'

'Okay. Shelley Adair is a friend.'

Shelley Adair! Rachel couldn't help but recognise the name of the internationally known model.

'Who you just happen to sleep with,' she said, wondering why they were even having this conversation. For pity's sake, a man who'd shared Shelley Adair's bed could have no serious interest in her. Beyond a minor curiosity, that was.

'It might interest you to know that I haven't slept with another woman since the morning I kissed you in your kitchen back home,' Joe retorted. 'Damn it, Rachel, what do you think I am?'

Rachel couldn't answer that. Instead she said quietly, 'I think you're a very attractive man. And if it's any consolation at all, being with you was—incredible. I've never...' But she broke off at that point, realising she could hardly confess that being with Steve had never been like being with him. Joe was Steve's friend, after all. 'I've had a wonderful evening.'

Joe groaned. 'So why are you running out on me now?'

'You know why.'

'Because you want commitment?' For the first time the word didn't stick in his throat.

'No!' Rachel backed all the way to the door. 'I don't expect anything like that from you.' She shook her head. 'Joe, it was good, really good, but we live in different worlds, you know that.'

'How different?'

Rachel gazed at him helplessly. 'You know how. I don't have homes all over the world. I don't drive expensive cars or fly around in private planes.' She spread her hands. 'Believe it or not, I wouldn't want to. I'm—I'm quite happy with my life. I have my daughter, I have my work. I don't need anything else.'

'I don't believe that.'

'Well, that's the way it is.'

'No.' Joe's scowl deepened. 'For God's sake, Rachel, at least admit that you wanted me.'

Rachel bent her head, unable to meet his anguished gaze any longer. 'I'm not saying I didn't,' she muttered in a low voice. 'Oh, please, Joe, call me a taxi. Let me go back to the hotel.'

The pulse at Joe's temple beat a crazy tattoo, and before he could stop himself, he said harshly, 'All right. You want commitment, I'll give you commitment! Marry me! Stay in Florida as my wife!'

CHAPTER FOURTEEN

JOE flew into a private airfield north of Miami. Emerging from the airport buildings, he was relieved to find Luther waiting for him with the limousine. He had rung the chauffeur from the Jetstream and supplied him with his expected time of arrival, but it was always good not to encounter any problems at the end of what had been a rather harrowing trip.

'You okay, sir?' asked Luther with some concern as Joe slid into the back of the vehicle, and Joe pulled a wry face before replying.

'I've been better,' he admitted, glad to escape the humidity outside the car. His father suffering a stroke had not been something he'd ever expected, and although the old man was now on the road to recovery, it had been a worrying couple of weeks.

'And Mr Mendez?' the chauffeur added as they slipped into the traffic heading for downtown. 'Mr Napier said he'd heard he was out of the hospital, which must be a relief.'

'It is.' Joe nodded. 'Thankfully, it was only a minor attack. His doctors say there's no reason why he shouldn't be as good as new in time.'

'That's good to hear.' Luther had worked for the family for over twenty years, and both Joe and his father appreciated his loyalty. 'So are we heading for the office?'

'No.' Joe's jaw compressed. 'Take me to the condo, will you, Luther? I've got some personal business to attend to.'

'Yes, sir.'

Luther never questioned his instructions, and not for the first time Joe was grateful for his perspicacity. After all, there was no practical reason for him to be back in Florida only two weeks after he'd left, and Luther must know that. Bill Napier, the managing director of the Miami division of the company, didn't need him to hold his hand.

So why was he here?

Joe had no desire to answer that question. When he'd left here, despite the seriousness of his journey, he'd been heartily glad to be putting as many miles between himself and Rachel as he could. After what had happened at the house on Biscayne Bay, he'd needed the objectivity that distance usually provided. It annoyed the hell out of him that he was back here now with no more impartiality than he'd had when he left.

Telling Luther he wouldn't need him any more that day, Joe took one of the high-speed lifts to the penthouse floor. He liked the condo. It was fairly small—just four bedrooms—and convenient, but it wasn't home. He had two houses he called home: one in Eaton Court Mews in London, and the other an elegant brownstone on the Upper East Side of Manhattan.

Marla met him in the high-ceilinged entry. 'Mr Mendez!' she exclaimed warmly. She, too, had been informed of his return. 'It's good to see you again, Mr Mendez. Ah, but you look so tired! How is your father? Much better, I hope?'

'Much better,' agreed Joe, tugging off the tie he'd worn to his interview with his father's specialist that morning. His parents were living in New York for the summer, and his father had been treated at one of the major facilities in the city.

'But you are still worried about him, no?' fussed Marla, following him into the spacious living room. 'You should have stayed in New York, Mr Mendez. Whatever problems they are having at the Miami office could surely wait until your father is out of danger?'

'He is out of danger,' said Joe tolerantly. 'And there is no problem at the Miami office.' He paused. 'That's not why I've come back.'

'Ah.' Marla looked puzzled. 'So how long are you staying? If you are just here for a few hours—'

'I'll be staying longer than that,' Joe told her flatly, wishing she was more like Luther. Marla always had too much to say for herself. She treated him more like a surrogate son than an employer.

Her dark brows arched now, and Joe knew she was waiting for him to explain. 'There's someone I have to see,' he said, giving in with some impatience. Then, more briskly, 'I've had lunch. I'll let you know if I'll be in to dinner.'

'Yes, sir.' Marla lifted a careless shoulder and moved towards the door. Then she halted. 'Oh, I almost forgot, Mr Carlyle called yesterday afternoon. I told him you were not here, that you were still in New York.' She hesitated. 'I don't think he believed me.'

Joe paused in the middle of unbuttoning his shirt. 'What do you mean, he "called"? Did he phone? Is that what you're saying?'

'No.' Marla looked offended now. 'He *called*. From the lobby downstairs. I told him you were not here, and—'

'Yeah, yeah.' Joe didn't need a rerun of that particular part of the conversation. He frowned. 'Why do you think he didn't believe you?'

'I don't know.' Marla shrugged. 'I get these feelings sometimes.'

'And he didn't say anything else?'

'Oh, yes.' Marla could be very annoying at times. 'He asked if I knew where Mrs Carlyle was.' She huffed a little. 'As if anyone should know that better than him, eh?'

Joe could feel his nerves tightening. 'And that's all he said? Did you know where Mrs Carlyle was?'

'I think so.' Marla considered. 'I told him I hadn't seen Mrs Carlyle since she came here with him that evening over two weeks ago.'

Joe's patience stretched. 'And?' he prompted.

'And nothing.' Marla spread her hands. 'But if you ask me he and Mrs Carlyle are having problems, yes. Why else would he come here and practically accuse you of kidnapping his wife?'

'Oh, come on.' Joe stifled an oath. 'I think that's an exaggeration, don't you?'

All the same, he didn't like the idea that Steve and Lauren might have split. A pulse throbbed in his temple at the thought that Steve might be heading back to England in the not too distant future. If Steve and Lauren were having problems— and, remembering the way she'd behaved with him, it wasn't beyond the realms of possibility—Ted Johansen, as Lauren's father and a major shareholder in the company, might well insist that his contract be terminated.

Marla shrugged when he didn't say anything more, and after she'd left him Joe wandered over to the windows and stared out at the sunlit ocean creaming onto the beach below. Looking at the placid scene, it was hard to think how it must have looked a couple of weeks ago. When a tropical storm had hit the coast some miles north of the city, its backlash had been felt as far south as the Everglades.

But Joe hadn't been here to see it. He'd just had news of his father's collapse and had been heading north at the time. His mind had been full of the anxiety he was feeling for both his father and his mother, the responsibilities he had as their only male offspring weighing heavily on his shoulders.

Of course, as soon as he'd assured himself that his father's condition was stable, as soon as he'd satisfied himself that his mother and his sister—who'd flown over from California—

were coping, he'd found himself reliving everything that had happened at the house on Biscayne Bay.

In hindsight, he knew he'd behaved recklessly; no woman—least of all a woman like Rachel—would have taken his proposal seriously. It had been said in the heat of the moment, and Rachel had treated it with the contempt it deserved.

The trouble was, he hadn't seen it that way at the time. Despite an initial sense of relief when she'd refused his offer of marriage, he'd been angered that she could dismiss it so casually. Damn it, he'd never proposed to a woman before, and he'd felt insulted when she'd practically thrown it back in his face.

But—and it was a big 'but'—that hadn't prevented him from making arrangements to return to Florida as soon as his father was home from the hospital. He'd tried to tell himself that his main reason for coming back was to see Daisy again, to assure himself she was making satisfactory progress. Despite the fact that her mother had refused his offer of accommodation, he had arranged with Dr Gonzales that they should stay on at the clinic until Daisy was well enough to go home. But in his heart of hearts, he knew he couldn't wait to see Rachel again. He had to see her, he thought grimly. If only to convince himself that she'd saved him from making the biggest mistake of his life.

He turned abruptly away from the windows, aware that that assertion had a distinctly hollow ring. That despite the fact that he'd only known the woman for a few weeks, his proposal hadn't been as reckless as he was trying to claim. Okay, she was different from the women he was usually attracted to, but perhaps that was part of her appeal. There was no doubt that the notion of marrying anyone hadn't even been in his thoughts when he'd turned up at her house that morning four weeks ago. Yet for some reason the idea had grown on him, and although he was trying to dismiss it, the fact was it wouldn't go away.

Which was ridiculous, he told himself. And sad. He had to get Rachel out of his life for good and resume his normal existence. She'd disrupted his routine, sure, but he wasn't cut out for marriage. Not yet, anyway. He certainly wasn't cut out to be any kid's stepfather, and to imagine Daisy calling him 'Dad' was simply beyond belief.

All the same, he was looking forward to seeing the girl. She'd been quite a character, and he'd been flattered, admittedly, when she'd apparently accepted him into her life. But how she'd feel if he was going to marry her mother would be something else, he mused shrewdly. But then, he reminded himself again, that wasn't going to happen, so why was he even considering it?

He'd had a shower and was pondering whether or not he needed a shave when he heard voices coming from the living room. One was Marla's. It was unmistakeable. The other, also female, had an English intonation, and ignoring all the sane advice he'd been giving himself, Joe's heart leapt.

'Rachel,' he breathed, aware of a totally ridiculous lift of his spirits. Had she heard he was coming back to Miami? Without bothering to put on any clothes, he emerged from the bedroom wearing only a towel slung about his hips for decency's sake.

But it wasn't Rachel.

The two women had evidently heard his approach, and when he reached the living room door the younger turned from addressing Marla to give him a beaming smile.

'Darling!' Shelley Adair exclaimed, rushing across the room to fling her arms around his neck. Her glossy mouth sought his without hesitation, her thinly clad body pressed seductively to his, anticipating his response.

But Joe couldn't respond. Not in the way she expected, anyway. For the first time in his life, her alluring beauty left him cold. She'd obviously taken some trouble over her appearance; her filmy silk sheath clung to the slender lines of her body. But he realised, with a sense of disbelief, that he preferred a woman with more flesh on her bones, a woman who didn't regard her appearance as the most important factor of her life.

Yet, despite his instinctive withdrawal, Shelley didn't seem to notice. Or purported not to, at least. 'I've missed you so much,' she said, apparently putting his reticence down to Marla's presence. 'Have you missed me, darling? I know I couldn't wait until November to see you again. And when I had a couple of days free…'

Joe was hardly listening. Looking over Shelley's shoulder, he met Marla's eyes and knew she wasn't deceived. 'Um—make up one of the guestrooms for Ms Adair,' he said tightly. Then, easing himself away from Shelley. 'Give me a minute, will you? I'll just get dressed.'

'But Marla doesn't need to make up a room for me,' Shelley protested, her narrow brows drawing together as the possible reasons for his behaviour seemed to occur to her. 'I can share your room, can't I?' She gave a slightly nervous laugh. 'Unless you've got someone else in there?'

'No, I—' Joe found himself stumbling over the words. 'That is— Make up the guestroom, Marla. Ms Adair will tell you how long she's staying.'

Shelley's mouth had turned sulky now. 'What's going on here, Joe?' she demanded. 'Why are you being like this?'

'Would Ms Adair like a drink or some coffee?' suggested Marla, evidently doing her bit to ease the situation.

'Why don't you go and do whatever it was you were doing before I got here?' snapped Shelley, in no mood to be mollified by a housekeeper.

'And why don't you sit down and calm yourself while I get some clothes on?' said Joe, refusing to let her rile him. 'Thanks, Marla. You can go. I'll let you know if I need you.'

Marla, who also had a fiery temper, took his advice. But the door had hardly closed behind her before Shelley sprang into the attack again.

'What the hell do you mean, embarrassing me in front of your servant?' she demanded, almost stamping her foot in fury.

'We don't have servants in this country, Shelley,' said Joe mildly. 'Marla is my housekeeper. And you embarrassed yourself.' He paused. 'You should have phoned before you left England, and I'd have explained the situation. But as you're here, you're welcome to stay as long as you like.'

Shelley stared at him. 'So why am I being given the cold shoulder? I read about your father, and I'm sure it's been a difficult time for you. As a matter of fact, I was in two minds whether to fly to New York. But then I remembered you'd told me you were going to spend some time in Florida, and besides, I didn't want to intrude on your family at a time like this.'

'Yeah, well…' Joe was starting to feel chilled, and the beginning of a headache was probing like needles at his temples. 'As I say, the condo's yours if you want to use it. I'm leaving tomorrow anyway. I want to get back to New York.'

Shelley gasped. 'You're not serious!'

'I'm afraid I am.'

'But I've flown all this way just to spend some time with you.'

'I know, and I'm sorry.' But Joe knew there was little sympathy in his voice. 'You should have contacted me before you booked your flight. Naturally, I'll reimburse you for your ticket.'

Shelley sniffed. 'You think money can buy anything, don't you?' she choked.

'No.' But Joe suspected he had, until Rachel had proved him wrong.

'Well, you can keep your money,' said Shelley now. 'And you can shove your offer of the condo. I'm leaving, Joe, and if I walk out that door you'll never see me again.'

* * *

Rachel travelled home from London on the early-evening train.

She'd had a very successful day. The new book had been completed a week ago, and Marcia had rung to say the publishers had loved it. Today's lunch at the Ritz had been her way of thanking Rachel for allowing her to represent her. And although the book had proved harder to complete than either of her other two novels, evidently it hadn't affected her writing.

But now she was heading home again. And although she'd been initially buoyed by the compliments that had been paid her, as the shadows lengthened so too did her sense of isolation.

Which was ridiculous, really. She wanted to go home. Of course she did. If only to tell Daisy all about her day. She also wanted to see her face when she gave her the video iPod she'd bought for her in Oxford Street. It was like the one she'd insisted Daisy leave with the nurses for safe-keeping when she'd left the clinic. Rachel had been sure that they'd be happy to have the excuse to contact Joe again, particularly as he hadn't been around since that devastating night at the house on Biscayne Bay.

Daisy had been quite put out about it. Not knowing all the facts, she'd come to the conclusion that he'd got bored with her company. Were all men like her father? she'd asked Rachel, and Rachel's heart had ached for her daughter. Ached for herself, too, she acknowledged now. He'd obviously found something—or someone—else to keep him amused.

Thankfully, Daisy's condition had continued to improve, and Dr Gonzales had been extremely pleased with her progress. However, as Joe had suspected, it was another ten days before he allowed her to fly home to England.

Having rejected Joe's offer of accommodation, Rachel had been inordinately grateful when Dr Gonzales had offered them both rooms in the convalescent wing of the clinic. It had been so much better for Daisy than living in the stuffy confines of the *Park Plaza* hotel. Although Steve had visited his daughter again before he left, he and Lauren had departed for New York on schedule.

Daisy had gone back to school two days ago and was already a minor celebrity, according to her. Naturally, she'd glossed over her father's part in it. Instead, she'd concentrated on telling her friends how she'd flown in a private jet and spent time in a famous clinic. She'd had to tell them about her operation to excuse the hair that had been shaved from her head. But the Johansens' Miami mansion and their luxurious yacht had probably figured far more prominently than her tumble into the ocean.

It was cool outside the station. It was September, and already the nights were drawing in. Rachel looked about her, surprised to find that Howard and Daisy hadn't come to meet her. They usually did after one of her infrequent trips to London, but tonight there was no sign of Howard's modest car.

Trying not to worry—Daisy's health was always foremost in her thoughts—Rachel found a taxi and gave the driver her in-laws' address. Daisy was supposed to have gone there after school. Lynnie always gave her something to eat— Daisy was usually hungry—and then prepared a meal for when Rachel got home.

There was a strange car parked in the Carlyles' driveway, Rachel saw as she got out of the cab. Immediately her heart skipped a beat. Who could it be? she wondered anxiously. The Carlyles had few visitors. She prayed that nothing had happened to any of them. It looked suspiciously like the doctor's car.

She hurried up the path to the house. She had a key and she let herself into the hall without further ado. She could hear voices from the front room that was only used on special occasions. Her heart almost stopped altogether. Could it be Joe?

Then the sitting-room door opened and Evelyn stood on the threshold. Her face was flushed and excited, and Rachel knew at once that it wasn't bad news she had to deliver. 'Come and see who's here!' she exclaimed, not allowing Rachel to take off her coat before pulling her into the room. 'It's Steve. Isn't that wonderful news?'

CHAPTER FIFTEEN

RACHEL slept badly.

It had been an exhausting day and she was tired, but her brain was too active to sleep. The scene in her mother-in-law's sitting room kept going round and round in her head, and no matter what she did she couldn't relax.

Steve had had no right to come crying to his mum and dad just because his marriage to Lauren had hit a bad patch, she brooded resentfully, and then chided herself for the thought. They were his parents, after all, not hers.

All the same, it was hard for her to feel any sympathy for him. This was the man who'd walked out on her and Daisy nine years ago, who'd abandoned his wife and daughter in favour of a much younger woman. He'd had no sympathy for them then. He'd virtually cut them out of his life.

She was up at six, making herself a cup of coffee, when Daisy appeared in the kitchen doorway. Like Rachel, she wasn't dressed, and judging from the puffy circles around her eyes, she hadn't slept too well either.

'Hi,' she said, sliding in and slumping down into a chair at the table. 'May I have some of that?'

Rachel looked surprised. 'Since when have you liked coffee?'

'It's okay.' Daisy was dismissive. 'I had some when I was staying with Dad and Lauren. They don't drink tea, you know?'

'Don't they?' Rachel would have preferred not to think about Daisy's father. 'Oh, well, it's what you're used to, I suppose.'

'Mmm.' Daisy put her elbows on the table and rested her chin on her hands. 'I suppose I could have had tea if I'd wanted, but it was easier just to go with the flow.'

Rachel nodded. 'Well, the kettle's boiled, so you can please yourself. If you'd prefer tea, I'll make you a cup.'

Daisy lifted her shoulders. 'I don't really care.' She paused. 'Perhaps I'll just have orange juice. Is that all right?'

Rachel sighed. 'Daisy, you can have whatever you like.'

'Okay.' Daisy sounded a little miffed now and, getting up from the table, she went to get the carton of orange juice from the fridge. 'Whatever.'

Rachel watched as the girl filled a glass with the juice, and then when Daisy resumed her seat at the table, she poured her coffee and joined her. 'So,' she said brightly, 'You're up early.'

Daisy pulled a face. 'So're you.'

'Yes.' Rachel took a sip of the coffee, savouring the flavour of the beans. Then, deciding to take the bull by the horns, 'Didn't you sleep well?'

Daisy shrugged. 'Did you?'

'No.' Rachel sighed. 'I had a really bad night, actually.' She grimaced and then added with rather less discretion, 'So what's new?'

Daisy frowned. 'Don't you usually sleep well?'

'Oh…' Rachel didn't want to worry her daughter. Daisy didn't need to know that she hadn't slept well since that night at Joe's house. 'I sleep okay. How about you? Have you got a headache? Is that why you're up so early?'

'No.' Daisy shook her head. 'And if you're still worrying about my operation, don't. I hardly ever feel it now.'

'That's good.'

'Yes.' Daisy still looked troubled. 'But I didn't sleep very well either.' She paused, drawing her upper lip between her teeth and gazing at her mother with anxious eyes. 'It's just—' She broke off for a moment and then the words came in a rush. 'If—if Dad comes back to live in England, will I have to live with him?'

The air left Rachel's lungs on a gasp. 'What?'

'I said, if Dad—'

'Yes, yes.' Rachel had to stop her from repeating it. 'Daisy, why would you ask a thing like that? What has your father been saying to you?'

'It wasn't him,' muttered Daisy unhappily. 'It was Grandma. When I went to help her carry the tea things in from the kitchen, she said that if Dad and Lauren didn't get back together he might decide to stay here.'

'I see.' Rachel took another mouthful of her coffee to give herself time to think. She might have known Evelyn had something like this in mind. She'd been so excited when she'd opened the sitting-room door. 'Well…' She tried to be impartial. 'He might stay here.' Although she doubted it, remembering that Steve had moved to Miami to advance his career. 'But why would you think you'd be living with him?'

'Oh…' Daisy blew out a breath. 'Well, Grandma said if Dad was here I could live half the time with him and half with you.' She sniffed. 'But I don't want to live with him.'

Rachel felt shocked, but not really surprised. Evelyn had never given up hope of them getting back together, and this was probably her way of trying to engineer it.

'Look,' she said now, 'No one's going to force you to live anywhere. If you want to stay here, that's okay—but equally, if later on you want to spend time with your father, then that's okay, too.'

Daisy stared at her. 'Do you mean that?'

'Of course I mean it.' Rachel got up from her chair and went round the table to bend and give her daughter a reassuring hug. 'Daisy, all I want is what's best for you. Don't you know that?'

'Oh, Mum!' Daisy turned and buried her face against her mother's neck. 'I love you.'

'And I love you too,' said Rachel, feeling tears prickling behind her eyes. 'Now, drink your orange juice and I'll make us both some breakfast.'

Daisy sighed. Then, after taking a healthy swallow of the juice, she said thoughtfully, 'Mum, do you ever wonder why Mr Mendez didn't come to see me before I left the clinic?'

Rachel was glad she could blame the heat of the pan for her suddenly flushed cheeks. 'Of course not,' she said impatiently. *Just every other day!* 'Scrambled eggs all right?'

'Well, I know why,' declared Daisy smugly. 'Dad told me. Well, he told all of us, actually. What with Mr Mendez coming to see Grandma and Granddad before he went back to Florida and them knowing him too.'

Rachel swallowed. 'Really?'

'Yes, really.' Daisy eyed her slyly. 'Do you want to hear why?'

No! Yes! Rachel forced herself to keep her attention fixed on the eggs. 'If you want to tell me,' she said, trying not to sound as agitated as she felt. 'Pass me a couple of plates, will you?'

Daisy grumbled, but she obediently got up and took two plates out of the cupboard. 'You're not really interested at all, are you?' she muttered. 'And I thought you liked Mr Mendez.'

'I did. I do.' Rachel wondered how Daisy would feel if she told her how much. 'Go on. I am interested, honestly.' *Honestly!*

Daisy handed over the plates and then she said, 'His father was taken ill. Dad said he had to rush back to New York to be with him.'

Now she had Rachel's whole attention. 'His father?' she echoed faintly. 'Are you sure about this?'

'Mmm.' Daisy nodded, apparently pleased that she'd surprised her mother at last. 'And you know what else?'

Rachel hardly dared ask. 'No.'

'Mr Mendez was the one who arranged for us to stay at the clinic until I could come home.'

'*No!*' Rachel was stunned. 'How do you know all this?' she demanded, the pan of eggs forgotten.

'Dad told—'

'Yes, but why would your dad tell you something like that?'

Daisy shrugged. 'We'd been talking about me having the operation, and Grandma said how good it was of Dr Gonzales to let us stay on at the clinic.' She paused. 'Dad laughed, and said Gonzales couldn't afford to do a thing like that. He said Mr Mendez had arranged it before he left for New York.'

'Oh, Daisy!' Rachel didn't know what to say, what to think. After the way she and Joe had parted that night, she'd never have expected him to care what happened to them. But he had. And the knowledge tore aside the fragile veneer of indifference she'd worn since she'd got home.

'Mum?' Daisy sensed that something she'd said had upset her mother. 'What's the matter, Mum? It was kind of him, wasn't it? Well, I thought it was, anyway, after the way you described that hotel.'

'No— I mean, yes, it was kind of him. Very kind.'

'So why are you looking so weepy? Are you going to cry?'

'Don't be silly!' Rachel sucked in a breath. 'Of course I'm not going to cry. It's just that— Oh God!' The smell of burnt eggs had come to her nostrils, and she turned back to find them smoking in the pan. 'Damn!' She sniffed hard, but this time she couldn't prevent the tears from spilling down her cheeks. 'These are ruined!'

'It doesn't matter.' Daisy hurried forward to take the pan off the heat. 'We can have cereal or toast. I'm not very hungry. Are you?'

'Not very.' Rachel tore a kitchen towel from the roll and used it to blot her eyes. 'I'm sorry. I should have been watching what I was doing.'

'I distracted you.' Daisy scraped the remains of the eggs into the waste disposal and plunged the pan into the sink. Then she cast her mother another doubtful look. 'You did like Mr Mendez, didn't you?' she added shrewdly. 'That's why you're upset.'

'I'm not upset,' said Rachel, but Daisy didn't look as if she believed her.

'Do you think we'll ever see him again?' she asked. 'I wish we could. I really liked him, and I think that he liked me.'

'I think he liked you too,' said Rachel, recovering her control. 'Now, what's it to be? Cereal or toast?'

Daisy frowned, but when she spoke it wasn't to state her choice of food. 'He's not like Lauren,' she said, and Rachel didn't know whether to be relieved or sorry. 'I mean, he's got plenty of money, hasn't he? But he doesn't go on about it like she does. She is such a pain. Did I tell you what she said about me being fat? She said I'd have to watch what I eat for the rest of my life.'

Rachel managed a smile. 'Obviously Lauren hasn't heard of puppy fat. In a couple of years, you'll be as slim as she is. And you have to admit, Lauren is a beautiful woman,' she added drily, doubting Lauren would have been as generous about her.

'She's not as pretty as you,' retorted Daisy staunchly. 'And I don't want to be as skinny as her. I suppose Mr Mendez likes skinny women, doesn't he?' Her eyes widened suddenly. 'Do you think he's the reason she walked out on Dad?'

It was a possibility that hadn't occurred to Rachel until Daisy voiced it. But she thought about it a lot in the days and nights to come. According to Daisy, her father had told his parents that Lauren had left the Johansens' mansion just a few days after Joe had left for New York. He hadn't mentioned Joe, of course. But like Daisy, Rachel could see the connection.

During the following week, Rachel avoided all Evelyn's

attempts to bring her son and her ex-daughter-in-law together. Naturally, she expected Daisy to spend time with her father, and Rachel had no problem with that. But she herself had no desire to listen to any more of Steve's self-pity. His parents had sympathy for him. He was their only child, after all. But she didn't have to share their feelings—not when his selfishness had had such a dramatic effect on all their lives.

Then, the following Friday, she arrived home from the supermarket to find a disturbingly familiar vehicle parked at her gate. It was the four-by-four Joe had been driving when he'd come to her house before. A sleek black SUV with tinted windows and alloy wheels.

Rachel's heart skipped a beat. Then skipped another as she parked her car and the driver's door of the SUV was pushed open. It was Joe. She knew that even before he thrust a long, powerful leg out of the car. She felt it in her bones, she thought, trying to control her breathing. It was like a visceral recognition that sapped her strength and left her feeling weak and vulnerable.

She watched from the safety of her car as he got out and gave an involuntary stretch, as if he'd been sitting there for quite some time. The action separated the hem of his black tee shirt from low-slung jeans, exposing a muscled wedge of brown skin. And just the sight of him made her realise how much she'd longed to see him again.

Then he turned and looked at her, and she knew she couldn't sit there any longer. Thrusting open her door, she followed his example, making an event of locking the car before starting along the pavement towards him.

'This is a surprise,' she said, striving for normality. Then, as a thought occurred to her, 'Are you looking for Steve?'

Joe's brows descended. 'Is he here?' he demanded in a harsh voice, and a shiver slid down Rachel's spine.

'No,' she said quickly, wondering if he'd already tried

Steve's parents. 'Have you been to the Carlyles'? He's staying with them.'

Joe's mouth tightened. 'As if I care,' he said, nodding towards the house. 'Shall we go inside?'

Rachel swallowed. 'You're not looking for Steve?'

'No, I'm not looking for Steve,' he agreed grimly. 'Now, in your own time…'

Rachel hesitated, tempted to point out the flaws in his attitude. But then, deciding there was no advantage in provoking a sharper reprimand, she opened the gate and went up the path to the door.

The house was cool. She'd lowered the thermostat before leaving for the supermarket, and she wondered if he felt the chill. As he was only wearing a tee shirt, and he'd recently come from a much warmer climate, surely he had to notice the difference in temperature?

But that wasn't her concern, she reminded herself, and leading the way into the sitting room, she said brightly, 'Have you been waiting long?'

'Long enough.'

Joe was curt. He paused in the doorway, making no attempt to take up her offer to sit down, and she decided he was still nursing a grievance over what had happened the last time they'd been together.

'Um—Steve said your father was ill,' she ventured when the silence between them lengthened to uncomfortable proportions. 'How—how is he now?'

'Much better.' Another monotone response.

'That's good.' Rachel wrapped her arms about her midriff, realising she was feeling the cold even if he wasn't. 'Was it something serious?'

'A stroke.' Joe regarded her with dark, brooding eyes. 'Didn't Steve tell you that?'

'No.' Rachel moistened her lips. 'Actually, I've hardly seen

Steve since he got back. Daisy has, of course, but he and I—
Well, we don't have a lot to talk about.'

'Don't you?' Joe arched those dark brows now, and there
was a trace of cold mockery in his gaze. 'As I understand it,
Steve still has feelings for you.'

'What?' Rachel was astounded. Then a thought occurred
to her. 'Did Lauren tell you that?'

Joe didn't immediately reply, and her nerves stretched
alarmingly. Of course, she thought. Whatever he said, he was
here to ascertain the situation so far as Lauren was concerned.
And if that meant getting the facts from her instead of Steve,
then so much the better.

'As a matter of fact, Lauren's father told me what happened,' Joe said at last. 'According to him, Lauren found out
you and Steve had been spending a lot of time together while
Daisy was in the clinic.'

'That's ridiculous!' Rachel gasped. 'He and Lauren were
away for most of the time we were there.'

'Oh, yeah.' Joe realised that, in his fury at discovering
what he'd thought was her duplicity, he'd forgotten all about
that. 'So it's not true?'

'Of course it's not true.' Rachel was staggered that he
should think it was. 'In any case, why does it matter to you?'
She paused, and then said what she was thinking. 'Unless you
want Lauren for yourself.'

'Give me a break!' Joe stared at her disbelievingly and then
shook his head. 'I'm not interested in Lauren! I don't even like
the woman.'

Rachel felt totally confused. 'Then *why* are you here?'

'For pity's sake!' Joe stifled an oath. 'Why do you think
I'm here? I came to see you, Rachel. No one else. For some
reason…' He lifted a hand and squeezed the back of his neck.
'For some reason, I can't get you out of my head.'

Rachel felt a quiver begin in the pit of her stomach and

spread down into her legs. A trembly, achy feeling enveloped her and she badly wanted to sit down. *This couldn't be happening*, she thought. Or, if it was, it was for all the wrong reasons.

That night in Miami, she'd known he wanted her. Damn it, she'd wanted him, and for the first time in her life she'd acted without considering the consequences. And because it had been so good, she had to believe he wanted her now. But she had no intention of being another of his conquests— someone he could seduce and discard as soon as the next attractive prospect came along.

Yet, looking at him, it was incredibly hard to think sensibly. What woman wouldn't be flattered that a man like him would fly all the way over the Atlantic to see her again? Okay, she knew he had homes in London and New York, and he probably hadn't made the trip just to see her. But he was here—tall, dark and incredibly sexy—and her limbs turned to water at the memory of what making love with him had been like.

He was staring at her, his eyes dark and intent, and she knew she had to say something. Something that would prove to him she'd meant what she'd said in Miami. Something that would stop him from touching her and discovering what a terrible liar she was.

'Um—well, I'm very flattered,' she said at last, grateful that he'd moved out of the doorway while he was speaking and was no longer blocking her only means of escape. 'But—you know—I told you before, this isn't going to work.'

'Why not?'

He took a step nearer and Rachel moved behind the sofa, anxiously calculating the distance to the door. 'You know why not,' she said, keeping her tone matter-of-fact. 'I thought I explained the situation that night in Miami.'

'The night you rejected my proposal of marriage?' suggested Joe harshly, and Rachel edged a little nearer to the door. 'It wasn't a real proposal of marriage,' she protested. 'You know that as well as I do. You wanted your own way and you weren't getting it. I think you said the first thing that came into your head.'

'No!' Joe was very definite about that. 'Believe me, offering marriage is not the first thing that comes into my head when I'm with a woman.'

'I believe you.' Ridiculously, Rachel felt a little offended now. Abandoning any attempt to be subtle, she quickly walked towards the door. 'That was why I didn't take you seriously,' she added stiffly. She glanced back over her shoulder. 'I think you ought to go.'

She'd only taken a couple of steps across the tiles when he came after her. Catching the sleeve of the knitted woollen jacket she'd worn to go out in, he practically dragged it off her shoulders in his haste. Then he swung her round and pushed her back against the wall of the hall behind her.

He wasn't gentle. There was a roughness to his actions that was reflected in the dark eyes that raked her startled face. 'This isn't over,' he said harshly, cupping her chin in a surprisingly callused hand. Then he bent his head towards her and his mouth came hungrily down on hers.

As always, when he touched her, Rachel's limbs turned to water. It was so much easier to think sensibly when her mouth wasn't locked with his. She closed her eyes, lost in a web of sensation that was so pleasurable, so erotic, that her head swam with it. The tactile delight of his tongue in her mouth caused an actual pulse to beat between her legs.

'You drive me crazy,' he muttered at last, drawing back to look down at her with smouldering eyes. His thumb scraped possessively over her lower lip. 'And God knows you don't give me any encouragement.'

Rachel swallowed, the room steadying as the realisation of what she was doing brought a return of sanity. 'I won't be your mistress, Joe,' she said shakily. 'And if that's why you're here, you're wasting your time.'

'Am I?' He trailed one hand down her throat to the demure neckline of her cotton shirt, and she couldn't prevent a shiver of anticipation. Her skin pebbled and his mouth twisted in satisfaction. 'So, you don't like me to do this?' he suggested, dipping his hand inside her shirt and allowing two fingers to probe inside her bra. Her nipple hardened automatically, and a smile replaced the smug expression on his face. 'Really?'

'Yes,' she choked, knowing there was no point in denying it. 'Yes, I don't deny you can make me want you. But—but that's not the point.'

'What is the point, then?' demanded Joe, his tone hardening perceptibly. 'I've proved that we want each other. Isn't that enough?'

'No.' She tried to push him away from her, but he wouldn't let her. 'Joe, be sensible! I'm older than you.'

'Only a little.'

'I've got a child.'

'So what?'

She shook her head. 'You're not being reasonable. I—I can't be as irresponsible as you.'

'I'm not asking you to be irresponsible,' said Joe huskily. His hand found the button at the waist of her jeans and he opened her zip. Then, resisting her attempts to stop him, he slipped his hand between her legs. 'As I say,' he added a little unsteadily, 'I've proved that you want me. You can't deny it when I can feel how much.'

Rachel trembled. 'Please, Joe…'

Joe gazed down at her for a long, disturbing moment, and then he removed his hand and put both arms around her. He pulled her to him, her jeans slipping dangerously low on her hips as he did so. 'Okay,' he said, giving in to the urge to kiss the vulnerable curve of her neck. 'If you insist on waiting until our wedding night, then so be it.' He lifted his head, his lips tilting teasingly. 'I won't force you, even if we both know who would win.'

Rachel could only stare at him. 'You don't mean that,' she protested.

'That I won't force you? Of course, I—'

'No! No, not that.' Rachel was impatient now, her small hands gripping his upper arms, keeping him away from her as if her life depended on it. 'Joe, don't joke about this. It's really not very funny.'

'Who's joking?' His dark brows arched in what she was sure must be mocking indignation. 'Okay.' He took a step backward and went down on one knee. 'If I have to beg, I'll do it. Rachel, will you do me the honour of becoming my wife?'

CHAPTER SIXTEEN

RACHEL felt tears pricking at the backs of her eyes. 'I—I wish you wouldn't do this,' she said, clutching her jeans around her waist. She took a deep breath, admitting defeat. 'All right. You've won. I'll go to bed with you. Now, please, get up. You look silly, kneeling there.'

'Well, thanks for that,' said Joe flatly as he rose to his feet. 'Do I take it you're turning my proposal down again?'

'Don't make fun of me, Joe,' said Rachel tremulously. 'I've said I'll go to bed with you and I will.' She glanced at her watch. 'Though not when Daisy's due home from school. I wouldn't like her to come home and find us together.'

Joe rocked back on his heels. 'Ah, well, there, you see, I can't agree to that.'

'Agree to what?'

'To us not being able to spend time in bed together when Daisy's around.'

'Joe—'

'No, listen to me.' He grasped her upper arms, all humour vanishing from his dark, arresting features. 'I love you, Rachel. Do you hear me? And I really do want to marry you. I want you, me, and Daisy to be a family. Well, for the time being,' he added as she gazed up at him with disbelieving eyes. 'If you're not too old,' his eyes twinkled, 'we might make another baby or two. If that's what you want, of course.'

Rachel took a shaky breath. 'You—love me?'

'Yes, I love you.' Joe took his hands from her arms and rested his palms against the wall at either side of her head. 'God knows why,' he added whimsically. 'You're not exactly good for my ego.'

'You don't need me to pay you compliments,' said Rachel, her mouth a little dry now.

Joe sucked in a gulp of air. 'Not exactly the response I wanted,' he told her tensely. 'Does that mean what I think it means?'

Rachel swallowed. 'And that would be?'

'Oh, you know.' Joe rolled his eyes. 'I'm good to go to bed with, but when it comes to choosing a life partner...'

'Don't!' Her anguished cry cut him off. With trembling fingers she cradled his face and then pressed her fluttering lips to his mouth. 'I love you. Why do you think I refused your first proposal? Because I couldn't bear for you to make fun of something so—so serious.'

'Ah, God!' Joe lowered himself against her, his mouth crushing hers with all the pent-up emotions he'd been denying for so long. 'I wasn't making fun,' he told her at last when he lifted his head. 'Okay, maybe I didn't want to admit it, even to myself, but I think I've loved you since that morning I came here to talk about Daisy's trip. But you're right about one thing: that night in Miami, I would have said anything to persuade you to stay.'

'Then—'

'Let me finish.' Joe allowed his knuckles to brush her anxious lips. 'When you refused to take me seriously, I was seriously ticked off. I thought, what the hell, I don't need this. That was why I let you go.'

Rachel frowned. 'So what made you change your mind?

If you have really changed your mind,' she added doubtfully, and Joe groaned.

'Oh, baby, I changed my mind about an hour after you'd left me.' He shook his head. 'I had every intention of seeing you again. Then I got that call from my mother, telling me my father was very ill, and I realised I was going to have to go away without resolving the situation between us.'

Rachel could hardly believe this was happening. 'So, have you been back to Florida since we came home?'

'Oh, yeah.' Joe was rueful. 'And believe me, I was pretty annoyed when I found you'd left the clinic without letting me know. Then, when I had Lauren's father ringing me, telling me that she was heartbroken because you and Steve had shut her out while Daisy was in the clinic, I felt even more aggrieved, I can tell you.'

'But that's not true!'

'I know, I know.' Joe's tongue touched the pulse palpitating below her ear. 'But you have to give me some credit for being bloody jealous.' He grimaced. 'You have to understand, I'd spoken to Daisy's doctor before I left and ensured you'd have somewhere to stay until I got back—'

'Yes, I know,' she interrupted him a little breathlessly. 'Steve's parents had apparently said how grateful they were to Dr Gonzales for organising it, and he told them it was you who'd arranged it.' She shook her head. 'It was so kind of you.'

'It wasn't kind,' he interrupted now. 'Sweetheart, I needed to know you were somewhere safe, somewhere I didn't have to worry that one night some drunken jerk might try and force his way into your hotel room. The *Park Plaza*'s okay, but it doesn't have the most salubrious reputation, and I wanted to ensure you'd be waiting for me when I got back.'

'Oh, Joe.'

'Yeah, "oh, Joe",' he echoed drily. 'And then, when I heard Steve was back in England, naturally I thought the worst. I'm a man, what can I say? A man who doesn't care for the idea that his woman is seeing another guy.'

Rachel caught her breath. 'Am I your woman, Joe?'

'You are if you accept my proposal,' he said huskily. 'Which reminds me, I don't believe you've given me an answer yet.'

Rachel and Joe were married in New York just before Christmas. Joe would have liked the ceremony to happen sooner, but out of respect for his father, who'd naturally wanted to attend, he'd delayed the date for a couple of months. And as he'd ostensibly taken up residence at his London home—which meant he could spend most of his days and nights with Rachel—he'd had no real cause for complaint.

Rachel had been anxious about how Daisy would react to the news that Joe was to be her stepfather, but she needn't have worried. 'I knew you liked him!' Daisy had exclaimed triumphantly. 'As soon as I realised you and Dad weren't going to get back together, I hoped you'd find someone else. And Joe's really cool, isn't he? Not to mention loaded!'

'Daisy!' Rachel had stared at her daughter. 'I hope you don't think I'm marrying Joe because he's got lots of money?'

'No.' Daisy spoke grudgingly. 'I know you're far too goody-goody to do a thing like that.'

'Daisy!'

'Well.' Daisy had the grace to turn red. 'You are. I just hope Joe loves you as much as you love him.'

'He does.' That was something Rachel had no doubts about.

'I know.' Daisy sighed. 'Grandma's going to be so…' She broke off, and Rachel decided she didn't want to know the word her daughter had been about to use. 'Disappointed,' she added at last. 'I think she's still hoping you and Dad might get back together.'

Rachel hesitated. 'How about you?' she asked gently, and Daisy shrugged.

'I knew it wasn't going to happen. I remembered what you'd said before I went to Miami, and then when you met Joe again...'

'So you approve?'

'Mmm.' Daisy nodded. 'And Grandma will too, when she comes around.'

Rachel had wondered. Evelyn had been bitterly disappointed to learn that Rachel was going to marry someone else. It was probably just as well Steve was staying with them, because it had given both of them an excuse for not seeing one another.

But then, Lauren had rung and told Steve she was sorry she'd doubted him. No doubt she'd heard that Joe was going to marry Rachel, too, and had decided to cut her losses. In the event, Steve had taken off back to Miami with only a desultory word of farewell for his daughter, and Evelyn had been forced to accept that what hopes she'd had were never going to be realised.

Another possible obstacle had been removed when Joe decided to take up permanent residence in England. 'This way, Daisy's education isn't going to suffer,' he'd said casually, making Rachel love him even more. 'We can always spend the holidays in the States. Then, when she's old enough, she can choose whether she wants to go to an English or an American university.'

'But won't that interfere with your work?' Rachel asked one morning after Daisy had left for school. Joe was still in bed, reading the morning papers, and she'd brought toast and a fresh pot of coffee upstairs for them to share. 'Your living here, I mean?'

'I've always spent a lot of time in England anyway,' said Joe, moving aside to allow her to climb onto the bed beside him. 'These days, much of what I do can be done by email or video-conferencing, and when I have to travel I'll arrange it so you can come with me.'

Rachel tucked the lapels of the fluffy cashmere dressing gown Joe had bought her closer about her. 'And can you do that?' she asked, sitting cross-legged so she could place the tray on the bed in front of her.

'Hey, I own the company,' said Joe teasingly. 'I get to do whatever I like.'

Rachel drew a trembling breath. 'Do you want coffee first or toast?'

Joe surprised her by lifting the tray and setting it on the bedside table at his side of the bed. 'I want you first,' he told her huskily, pulling her towards him. His hand slid down into the vee she'd made of her legs. 'Mmm, that's better,' he said, encountering warm flesh and damp curls. 'I want to love you,' he added, his tongue tracing the parted contours of her lips. 'Who needs food when I can eat you?'

They honeymooned in Hawaii, choosing one of the smaller islands where the tourists could be trusted to leave them alone. They spent four weeks relaxing and swimming and soaking up the sun. Rachel's skin turned a delicious honey-brown, and her hair was bleached to a flattering lightness.

Daisy spent the time with her two sets of grandparents.

Evelyn had come around, as Daisy had predicted, and she and Howard had been especially thrilled when Joe had flown them both to New York for the wedding ceremony.

'Can you imagine anyone else inviting his wife's ex-in-laws to his wedding?' Rachel had teased Joe when he'd asked her opinion. 'Oh, darling, I don't know what I've done to find someone as wonderful as you.'

'Just lucky, I guess,' Joe had said with a smug grin. Then, as she'd wound her arms about his waist, 'Hey, didn't you say Daisy was due home from school?'

Rachel had ignored him, and the kiss they'd shared had quickly deepened to a sensual assault on her senses.

Joe's parents had taken to Daisy at once. His mother had

told Rachel they were so relieved their son had fallen in love at last, and finding they had a ready-made granddaughter had been a bonus.

As far as Rachel was concerned, she'd loved Joe's parents on sight. His father was so like Joe, and his mother had instantly made her feel as if she was already part of the family.

Consequently, she had no qualms about leaving Daisy in their care for the first two weeks she and Joe were away. Snow was falling in the mountains upstate, and they were planning to take Daisy skiing, with trips to the Statue of Liberty, the Empire State Building, and shopping on Fifth Avenue thrown in for good measure. Then Joe's sister, Rosa, would escort her back to England for a two-week stay with Steve's parents.

On their last night in Hawaii, they went out to one of the small fish restaurants that were so popular in the resort where their hotel was situated. They ate lobster and clams, and Rachel was irresistibly reminded of the first meal they'd shared together in Miami.

She was gazing reminiscently into the distance when Joe captured her hand and brought it to his lips. 'Penny for them,' he said lightly. 'Or shall I guess?'

Rachel's green eyes softened as they turned to his dark face. 'Can you?'

'I think so.' His eyes darkened. 'We ate fish at the Sea House, and then I made love to you for the first time.'

'Hmm.' Rachel kissed his knuckles in her turn. 'It was the most perfect experience I'd ever had. I'd never felt like that before.'

'Not even with Steve?'

'No.' Rachel was definite.

Joe pulled a wry face. 'I used to think I'd never hear that guy's name without wanting to sock him on the jaw. But you know, I have so much to thank him for.'

Rachel dimpled. 'Do you think so?'

'Oh, yeah.' Joe's knee rubbed sensuously against hers. 'He did me the greatest favour in the world. He allowed me to meet you.'

Rachel took a deep breath. 'I doubt if he sees it that way.'

'Tough.' Joe was unrepentant. 'Now, I've got something to tell you.'

Rachel frowned. She had something to tell Joe, too, and she wondered for a moment if he'd guessed her secret.

But no. As he started to speak, she realised that what he had to tell her was just going to add to their happiness.

'You remember what I said about us needing somewhere larger to live now that I'm going to be working at home as well as you?' he asked, and she nodded.

'Well, I wonder how you'd feel about us buying a small estate just outside of Westlea. Melton Hall is up for sale, and I've got first refusal, if you're interested.'

Rachel caught her breath. 'Melton Hall?' she echoed. 'But that's enormous!'

'Not very.' Joe gazed at her appealingly. 'It has just eight bedrooms. And Charles says he'll come and organise the place for us, which is quite a concession. He's always insisted he'd never move out of London, but I think you and Daisy have won him over.'

'Oh, Joe.' Rachel stared at him in disbelief. 'I don't know what to say.'

'You could say you'll at least give the idea some consideration,' he murmured gently. 'What do you think?'

Rachel shook her head. 'I hope you're not thinking we'll be able to fill all those bedrooms!' she protested, and he gave a soft laugh.

'No. As I say, that's up to you. But there'll be you and me and Daisy. And Charles, of course. And my parents, when they come to stay.'

Rachel moistened her lips. 'Would you mind if there was someone else? Fairly soon, actually.'

Joe's brows drew together. 'You don't mean...?'

'Hmm.' She felt a ridiculous wave of colour sweeping up her throat. 'I'm pregnant.' She took a breath and then added quickly, 'I was going to tell you tonight. You—you just beat me to it.'

'Oh—my—God!' Joe gazed at her, his lips parting in stunned disbelief. Then his eyes dropped intimately to where her stomach disappeared beneath the rim of the table. 'You're going to have a baby. *My* baby. Oh, my God!'

Rachel swallowed. 'Are you pleased?'

Joe's fingers gripped hers so tightly she winced. 'Am I pleased?' he breathed, and ignoring the other diners, he leant across the table and gave her a long, lingering kiss. 'I'm ecstatic,' he told her at last. 'I love you, Rachel Mendez. And when we get back to our suite, I'm going to show you exactly how much.'

* * * * *

Here is a sneak preview of
A STONE CREEK CHRISTMAS,
the latest in Linda Lael Miller's acclaimed
McKETTRICK *series.*

A lonely horse brought vet Olivia O'Ballivan to Tanner
Quinn's farm, but it's the rancher's love that might cause
her to stay.

A STONE CREEK CHRISTMAS
Available December 2008
from Silhouette Special Edition

Tanner heard the rig roll in around sunset. Smiling, he wandered to the window. Watched as Olivia O'Ballivan climbed out of her Suburban, flung one defiant glance toward the house and started for the barn, the golden retriever trotting along behind her.

Taking his coat and hat down from the peg next to the back door, he put them on and went outside. He was used to being alone, even liked it, but keeping company with Doc O'Ballivan, bristly though she sometimes was, would provide a welcome diversion.

He gave her time to reach the horse Butterpie's stall, then walked into the barn.

The golden retriever came to greet him, all wagging tail and melting brown eyes, and he bent to stroke her soft, sturdy back. "Hey, there, dog," he said.

Sure enough, Olivia was in the stall, brushing Butterpie down and talking to her in a soft, soothing voice that touched something private inside Tanner and made him want to turn on one heel and beat it back to the house.

He'd be damned if he'd do it, though.

This was *his* ranch, *his* barn. Well-intentioned as she was, *Olivia* was the trespasser here, not him.

"She's still very upset," Olivia told him, without turning to look at him or slowing down with the brush.

Shiloh, always an easy horse to get along with, stood contentedly in his own stall, munching away on the feed Tanner had given him earlier. Butterpie, he noted, hadn't touched her supper as far as he could tell.

"Do you know anything at all about horses, Mr. Quinn?" Olivia asked.

He leaned against the stall door, the way he had the day before, and grinned. He'd practically been raised on horseback; he and Tessa had grown up on their grandmother's farm in the Texas hill country, after their folks divorced and went their separate ways, both of them too busy to bother with a couple of kids. "A few things," he said. "And I mean to call you Olivia, so you might as well return the favor and address me by my first name."

He watched as she took that in, dealt with it, decided on an approach. He'd have to wait and see what that turned out to be, but he didn't mind. It was a pleasure just watching Olivia O'Ballivan grooming a horse.

"All right, *Tanner*," she said. "This barn is a disgrace. When are you going to have the roof fixed? If it snows again, the hay will get wet and probably mold…"

He chuckled, shifted a little. He'd have a crew out there the following Monday morning to replace the roof and shore up the walls—he'd made the arrangements over a week before—but he felt no particular compunction to explain that. He was enjoying her ire too much; it made her color rise and her hair fly when she turned her head, and the faster breathing made her perfect breasts go up and down in an enticing rhythm. "What makes you so sure I'm a greenhorn?" he asked mildly, still leaning on the gate.

At last she looked straight at him, but she didn't move from

Butterpie's side. "Your hat, your boots—that fancy red truck you drive. I'll bet it's customized."

Tanner grinned. Adjusted his hat. "Are you telling me real cowboys don't drive red trucks?"

"There are lots of trucks around here," she said. "Some of them are red, and some of them are new. And *all* of them are splattered with mud or manure or both."

"Maybe I ought to put in a car wash, then," he teased. "Sounds like there's a market for one. Might be a good investment."

She softened, though not significantly, and spared him a cautious half smile, full of questions she probably wouldn't ask. "There's a good car wash in Indian Rock," she informed him. "People go there. It's only forty miles."

"Oh," he said with just a hint of mockery. "*Only* forty miles. Well, then. Guess I'd better dirty up my truck if I want to be taken seriously in these here parts. Scuff up my boots a bit, too, and maybe stomp on my hat a couple of times."

Her cheeks went a fetching shade of pink. "You are twisting what I said," she told him, brushing Butterpie again, her touch gentle but sure. "I meant..."

Tanner envied that little horse. Wished he had a furry hide, so he'd need brushing, too.

"You *meant* that I'm not a real cowboy," he said. "And you could be right. I've spent a lot of time on construction sites over the last few years, or in meetings where a hat and boots wouldn't be appropriate. Instead of digging out my old gear, once I decided to take this job, I just bought new."

"I bet you don't even *have* any old gear," she challenged, but she was smiling, albeit cautiously, as though she might withdraw into a disapproving frown at any second.

He took off his hat, extended it to her. "Here," he teased. "Rub that around in the muck until it suits you."

She laughed, and the sound—well, it caused a powerful

and wholly unexpected shift inside him. Scared the hell out of him and, paradoxically, made him yearn to hear it again.

* * * * *

Discover how this rugged rancher's wanderlust is tamed in time for a merry Christmas, in
A STONE CREEK CHRISTMAS.
In stores December 2008.

Virgin Brides, Arrogant Husbands

Demure but defiant...
Can three international playboys
tame their disobedient brides?

Proud, masculine and passionate, these men
are used to having it all. But enter Ophelia,
Abbey and Molly, three feisty virgins to whom
their wealth and power mean little. In stories
filled with drama, desire and secrets of the
past, find out how these arrogant husbands
capture their hearts....

Available in December

THE GREEK TYCOON'S DISOBEDIENT BRIDE

#2779

REQUEST YOUR FREE BOOKS!

2 FREE NOVELS
PLUS 2
FREE GIFTS!

PASSION GUARANTEED SEDUCTION

YES! Please send me 2 FREE Harlequin Presents® novels and my 2 FREE gifts (gifts are worth about $10). After receiving them, if I don't wish to receive any more books, I can return the shipping statement marked "cancel". If I don't cancel, I will receive 6 brand-new novels every month and be billed just $4.05 per book in the U.S. or $4.74 per book in Canada, plus 25¢ shipping and handling per book and applicable taxes, if any*. That's a savings of close to 15% off the cover price! I understand that accepting the 2 free books and gifts places me under no obligation to buy anything. I can always return a shipment and cancel at any time. Even if I never buy another book, the two free books and gifts are mine to keep forever.   106 HDN ERRW 306 HDN ERRL

Name	(PLEASE PRINT)	
Address		Apt. #
City	State/Prov.	Zip/Postal Code

Signature (if under 18, a parent or guardian must sign)

Mail to the **Harlequin Reader Service:**
IN U.S.A.: P.O. Box 1867, Buffalo, NY 14240-1867
IN CANADA: P.O. Box 609, Fort Erie, Ontario L2A 5X3

Not valid to current subscribers of Harlequin Presents books.

Want to try two free books from another line?
Call 1-800-873-8635 or visit www.morefreebooks.com.

* Terms and prices subject to change without notice. N.Y. residents add applicable sales tax. Canadian residents will be charged applicable provincial taxes and GST. Offer not valid in Quebec. This offer is limited to one order per household. All orders subject to approval. Credit or debit balances in a customer's account(s) may be offset by any other outstanding balance owed by or to the customer. Please allow 4 to 6 weeks for delivery. Offer available while quantities last.

Your Privacy: Harlequin Books is committed to protecting your privacy. Our Privacy Policy is available online at www.eHarlequin.com or upon request from the Reader Service. From time to time we make our lists of customers available to reputable third parties who may have a product or service of interest to you. If you would prefer we not share your name and address, please check here. ☐

HP08R

THE ITALIAN'S BRIDE

Commanded—to be his wife!

Used to the finest food, clothes and women,
these immensely powerful, incredibly
good-looking and undeniably charismatic
men have only one last need: a wife!

They've chosen their bride-to-be and they'll
have her—willing or not!

Enjoy all our fantastic stories in December:

THE ITALIAN BILLIONAIRE'S
SECRET LOVE-CHILD
by CATHY WILLIAMS (Book #33)

SICILIAN MILLIONAIRE,
BOUGHT BRIDE
by CATHERINE SPENCER (Book #34)

BEDDED AND WEDDED FOR REVENGE
by MELANIE MILBURNE (Book #35)

THE ITALIAN'S UNWILLING WIFE
by KATHRYN ROSS (Book #36)

HPE1208

HARLEQUIN *Presents*

Coming Next Month

Plus, look out for the fabulous new collection
The Italian's Bride, from Harlequin Presents® EXTRA: